# The Yellowstone Ranch

## Cloette Ribes

# Contents

# 1

----------------------------------------------------------------

The orange standing tape scratched my fingers as I wrapped it around the old horses legs. It's legs were swollen and retaining fluid but no tendon or ligament problems.

"We're down four horses, and I'm three wranglers short. There's no way we're gonna get all those fucking cattle loaded today. It's just not possible."

The voice sounded frustrated and impatient and maybe even a little hopeless. I looked up to see a man with long hair under a brown cowboy hat standing at the door way of the barn me and this horse were in. He leaned against the frame, facing out. He didn't even realize I was in here, he was too wrapped up in his own problems.

"I- yeah. Yeah, I get that... I'll let Rip know... He can get it done... Yeah...I've gotta take care of a problem out by McKinneys Ranch and then I'll be back...Alright. Bye." He shoved the phone in his pocket. "Fuck." I heard him quietly curse.

"If it makes ya feel any better you're only three horses short." I spoke up with a teasing and positive tone. He sounded like he needed some positivity.

He turned around. Confused at first. "Shit, I didn't even realize you were in here."

"No biggie." I smiled and finished wrapping her leg.

"Are you the new vet? I didn't realize Dr. Stone was..." his words trailed off.

"He's still- I'm not the new vet. He still practices. Just helping for the summer." I nodded, babbling  then put the horses leg back down. He was silent for a minute. Just watching.

"So she's good to go?" He cleared his throat.

I unbuckled her bridle from the wall and scratched between her eyes. "Good as gold. Just some extra fluid on her legs, no tendons tore or anything. Maybe cut her back on the sweet feed and give her a few beers tonight." I started to walk her back to her stall.

He chuckled a little. "Really?"

I stopped and turned back to look at him. A little smile formed on my lips, realizing I made him laugh although with no intention too. "Yeah, it'll help her sweat out that fluid."

He nodded,"Alright, good to know." I put the horse back in her stall and grabbed my bag to leave. "I didn't catch your name." The cowboy spoke up to me this time.

I smiled again and looked at the ground to hide my blush from this handsome man. I glanced back up to him. "It's Ada."

"Ada." He blinked slowly at me. Not smirking but not smiling. His brown eyes looked warm and kind.

"And yours is?" I chuckled at how he was acting. A way most men never acted around me.

He chuckled too,"Kayce."

Kayce. Kayce Dutton. Of course it is.

"I've heard about you." I nodded and swallowed. All the girls at the clinic talked about him. How hot the new livestock commissioner was. Everyone knew who he was. I was only here for a few days when I first heard of him and now within the month, I've met him.

He sighed and said with a breathy voice,"I'm sure. I'm nothing like what anyone has told you."

I smiled and decided it was okay to flirt. That he was interested in me too. "Damn," I blinked slowly,"I liked what I've heard." I slung my bag over my shoulder and started to walk out.

It wasn't completely a lie. All the girls, especially Hannah, made him sound dreamy but dangerous. All the stories of all he went through and how tough him and his family are. Mostly all the people they killed. They say Kayce is Johns hired hit man. How no one messes with them because they're all so loyal to one another and would do anything to keep each other safe. It was something I ached for since I was a kid.

I walked my way to the vets truck and jumped in. I put it in drive and took off back to the clinic.

I had plenty of time to let my mind wonder. What it would be like to have someone who cared and loved you so much they would stop at nothing to protect you. The story about Kayce that stuck out to me most was the first one I heard. About how his dad was shot and nearly killed and he tracked down the people that did it. And killed every one. But there were more stories. Like putting a man under a cattle guard and tying one to a fence. Making bikers dig their own graves and leaving trespassers in the middle of pastures surrounded by wolf bait.

I was more interested in the stories that the old men told at the clinic though. The ones about Kayce in Pakistan. They said he was a Navy Seal and went on extremely dangerous missions. It reminded me of my father, an Army Ranger who was KIA in Iraq. Who knows if any of the stories were real but they always intrigued me.

And then there were the other stories about his love affairs with the Native women nearby. Everyone says he definitely has a type. Saying that he dated one Native who was a wrangler at the ranch and married another who was a teacher. The girls say they got divorced because Kayce refused to cut ties with his family. Once again, it could all be rumors. Maybe. Hannah is the one who told me most of this and I trusted her. I had known her the longest out of anyone here. When I pulled into the clinic, everyone was gone from work. I walked inside and upstairs to the loft, where I would be residing for the next few months until school started back in the fall. If I go back to school. I hadn't decided if I wanted to finish out vet school. I was honestly tired of school.

"I was about to sent a search party out there for ya!" I heard my room-mate/co worker/long time best friend holler from the bathroom. She was the whole reason I was here. We met in vet school in Wyoming but this is where she was born and raised. She landed me this gig. It didn't take much for her to convince her dad that his clinic would need the extra help especially with him being sick.

"No need Hannah, I survived!" I teased.

She stepped out of the bathroom, wrapped in a towel. "How'd it go?" She started drying her blonde hair with a different towel.

I grinned and shook my head. "I see why y'all go on about the Dutton boys."

She threw the towel at me laughing,"Ada Jane! You told me this summer was all business."

I tossed the towel back then grabbed a beer from the fridge and broke it open. "I'm kidding." I gulped down some of the beer and wiped my mouth. "He was friendly though." I smiled.

She rolled her eyes,"Was it Jamie? God, please don't tell me it was that damn politician-"

"It was Kayce." I said quietly.

She stopped joking and gave me a serious look. "I told you about him..."

I sighed loudly,"I know. I know. But..." I walked over and flopped down on the couch, my scrubs swishing as I walked.

"But what? But nothing." She sat down by me. "He's trouble. Hell,"She threw her hands in the air,"He's more than trouble. He's dangerous."

I nodded and swallowed hard. "But he's pretty to look at." I teased and she rolled her eyes again, standing up and heading towards the bedroom.

"I've warned you!" She hollered at me.

"Pizza?" I yelled back.

"Yes ma'am."

I stripped down and stepped into the shower. I definitely didn't mind Montana. It was better than the summer heat in Texas. June in Montana felt like October in Texas. So I didn't have to worry about sweating and taking four showers a day.

It was never my plan to leave Texas. But here we are.

I ordered the pizza.

*****

"Ada?" My vet and Hannah's dad, Dr. Stone, stepped into the procedure room where I was drawing up shots for a goat with pink eye.

"Yeah?" I turned to him.

"There's a few horses at Dutton Ranch that need to be checked on. I dressed their wounds last week, probably just need to be changed. How did it go there yesterday?" He asked.

I quickly thought of Kayce. Excited, and hoping I would get to see him again today.

"Great. No tendinitis, just oedema."

"Good,"He nodded,"They scare most vets off out there," He chuckled,"Good to know I can send someone else out there besides me. Hannah refuses to go anymore."

I smiled, feeling some validation from Dr Stone. "I'll head out there as soon as I finish these shots."

"Thank you."

*****

I pulled the truck up by the barn and went to check on the horses. But as soon as I was through redressing one of their wounds, I heard a familiar voice in the distance.

"Tell him I need those horses yesterday. And if they're not here in the next two hours, we'll buy from some else."

It was Kayce. On the phone again. Soon he was stomping into the barn, and slinging open a stall door. Obviously pissed at something. The stall door of a horse who's dressings still needed to be checked and changed.

"I'm not finished with him yet." I spoke up from the stall I was in.

"Too fucking bad. I'm taking the goddamn horse and there's nothing some vet can tell me to change my m-" he barked but stopped once he saw me. "Ada. Fuck, I'm sorry."

I stood there, wide eyed, shocked by what he said and starting to realize why they couldn't keep a vet- or anyone really- around here. I swallowed hard, trying to keep from either bursting out into tears. Don't be baby, Ada. Seriously, now is not the time.

His face changed from pissed and frustrated to soft and tired. "I- I didn't realize it was you. I'm really sorry-"

I didn't realize I hadn't said anything. I was just staring at him. I popped in action and started over to the horse. "No, it's fine! Just let me check him out really quick and then you can have him." He stepped out of my way.

I assumed he would leave and find a new horse like the others I just finished, but he was watching me. The dressings were not clean and needed to be replaced. "It's gonna be a little bit. I'll have to redress him." I dusted my hands off on my scrub pants and squatted down to start unraveling the tape.

"Let me help." He bent over to my level and worked on the other leg.

"It's okay, really. You can take her, she's all set and healed." I gestured to the one I just finished up.

"Ada," He said in a caring tone that made me look up  at quickly,"Just let me." He nodded slowly in a way that made me agree with him.

"Okay." I whispered. I hurried to unravel and clean and rewrap. He did the same but by the time he finished one I was done with the third one.

I walked out of the stall and didn't say a word. I started packing my things back into my bag. I wanted to be out of there. It was awkward and embarrassing and I wanted to go home.

"Ada." He called out to me as I was walking back to my truck. I didn't stop. Just acted like I didn't hear him. I opened the truck door and started to step in but he grabbed the door. "Hey."

"Yeah?" I turned sharply to him.

"Why are you hurrying off?" He let out with a deep breath.

Why do you care? I wanted to ask. I wanted to roll my eyes and ask what his problem was. Because I'm trying to do my job but you were being a prick, was another answer. There's better things for me to do than stand around listen to you bitch on the phone. I shrugged,"I'm not." Was what came out. Good one, Ada. He tilted his head to the side with a look that said Really. And I couldn't do anything but stare at him. God, he was gorgeous. No wonder I couldn't tell him what I was thinking. Hannah would kill me right now.

"You wanna go out?" He asked quickly.

I nearly choked on my words,"What?" My face turned red. I don't even know this man. And all I've ever heard is not great things. He pressed his lips together and glanced at the ground then back at me.

"Yeah, that's kinda soon, huh?" He let out a small chuckle and rubbed the back of his neck. "Sorry." He nodded once and stepped back,"Be careful." Then he turned to walk away.

Be careful. It was probably something he told everyone but it was gesture that meant a lot to me. Enough to speak up.

"Wait!"

He turned around quickly.

"Where are you taking me?" I smiled. Pushing everything Hannah told me out of my head.

He chuckled and dropped his head then leveled it with me. "I'll pick you up tonight at 8."

"I'm staying at the loft above the clinic." I stepped into the truck.

"Alright, I'll be there." He nodded and walked off.

2

------------------------------------------------------------

"You're gonna kill me." I said the minute I stepped in the door of the loft.

Hannah looked up from her phone. She was sitting on the couch, Law and Order playing on the TV. She grabbed the remote and turned it down. "Kayce?" She asked with no emotion.

I nodded. "Technically this is your dads fault-"

"My dad did not tell you to fuck Kayce Dutton-" She started in.

"Whoa!" I cut her off quickly, "I did not fuck him!" My eyes were probably wider now than early.

She was silent. "Oh." She nodded. "Okay. Okay. Good. So, what'd you do?"

I tossed my bag up onto the kitchen island counter, "Told him I would go out with him."

"Great." She dropped her head in her hands, "Here we go."

"I know." I leaned on the counter and did the same. "I couldn't tell him no."

She sighed. "Okay. Okay." She repeated herself again. "Okay." She was panicking. Definitely panicking. "Okay." She looked up from her hands and over at me. "So what are you wearing?"

I scoffed a little. "You're not gonna kill me?"

She stood up and walked over to me. "Not yet. Kayce and Monica had a pretty rocky ending. Maybe she smacked some sense into him." She leaned onto the counter in front of me.

I nodded. "Yeah."

I hope so.

I showered and shaved and blow dried my hair. By then it was 7:30 and I was running out of time.

"What about this?" Hannah pulled out a cute long sleeved, flowy dress with red and white polka dots.

My jaw dropped,"When did you get that?" I let a piece of hair off the curling iron. It bounced up to a wave.

She shrugged,"Couple weeks ago."

"I don't wanna be over dressed. I feel like a dress is too much." I clamped the curler around another piece of hair then twisted and wrapped it up.

"Okay..." she ran back in her room for a few minutes. "This?" Shorts and a tank top.

"I'll freeze."

"Fucking Texas." She mumbled and went back in. And then came back out with the same outfit but a flannel.

"It's basic." I shut off the curling iron and sat it on the counter.

"It's 7:45, Ada! Pick something." She ran back into her room. I heard hangers being tossed and moved as I threw on a little make up. He had only seen me in scrubs and no make up and unwashed hair, so anything was an improvement really.

"How about this?" She was holding my favorite light washed wranglers and a simple white long sleeves with buttons at the top.

"Do you think it'll be okay?" I asked quietly. Realizing how nervous I was.

She smiled. "You look good in everything, girl." I smiled a little, thankful for someone like her. "But he ain't gonna care whatcha wearing, he just wants you naked."

"Hannah!"

I went with the dress. It was too cute not to. I paired it with some brown strappy sandals and chunky jewelry per usual.

Then there was a knock at the loft door.

"I'll get it." Hannah went running past me.

"Be nice!" I yelled and ran to my room to grab my purse.

"Kayce. Hi. How are you?" I heard her in the other room.

"Hey Hannah. I'm fine. How are you? How's your dad?"

I slung my purse over my shoulder and let out a deep breath. Here we go. I stepped out of my room and walked their way.

"Hey." I smiled at him.

But he didn't smile. He just stared. "Hey." Then we were quiet. I glanced at the ground quickly then pushed my hair behind my ear. "Uh... " He started to talking but lost words. He let out a small chuckle. "Sorry, I wasn't expecting..." he smiled bigger.

I felt my face get hot and knew it was turning red.

"Yeah, she usually looks homeless at work." Hannah broke the silence.

His eyes got big,"No, no I didn't mean it like that! I was just..." Hannah and I started to laugh. Her sense of humor was dry and heard to catch sometimes. He chuckled with us and shook his head. "Are you ready?" He asked in a voice I hadn't heard from him. A comfortable, casual voice. No specific emotion. Just his real voice.

I nodded and followed him out the door and down the stairs. "Call me!" Hannah yelled. I giggled but didn't say anything. I was nervous.

He opened the door for me to step outside. Then he opened the door to the truck for me. I couldn't help but smile. It was something no one had ever done for me. He jumped into the drivers side and started the truck. Then off we went.

"I didn't put two and two together when you said you lived above the clinic." He mentioned after a few silent moments.

I started to just nod but realized I should probably open up and not be awkward. "Yeah, I met Hannah in vet school. She said Dr. Stone was needing the help this summer for large animals."

"I see," He nodded,"I'm surprised she let you come with me." He glanced over then back at the road.

I smiled,"She was hesitant."

"Me and her brother use to be close. We were all good friends as kids." He stared straight this time.

Brother? Hannah never mentioned a brother.

"Really?" I asked.

"Yeah, and then when..." He let out a sighed,"Everything happened..." He shook his head,"Hannah just... stopped coming around. For good reasons."

What was everything. Oh god, what have I gotten myself into.

"I'm sorry." I looked over at him.

He looked at me. His eyebrows a little ruffled. And just nodded, back to the mysterious and serious Kayce again.

"Why don't you guys have a vet at Yellowstone?" I changed the subject quickly.

He propped his arm up on the center console,"We've tried. Can't get anyone that wants to work their life away."

"Sounds about right." I chuckled. "No one wants work anymore."

"Seems like you do. Just horses?" He turned the truck onto a highway. I wasn't sure which one or where it went. I didn't ever leave our little area of work.

"Uh no," I cleared my throat,"Large animals. Cattle, horses, goats, mules, donkeys. The donkeys are my favorite." A smile grew on my face thinking of the adorable, gentle creatures.

He chuckled,"Oh yeah?"

I nodded and couldn't help but look at him again. Admiring the smile I put on his face under the handle bar mustache. I realized the hat he had on now was different than what I had previously seen. This one was black and spotless. And the denim shirt he was wearing looked iron and the jeans looked starched. I wasn't the only one trying to impress someone.

He looked over at me with half a smile. I let out a small chuckle and looked back forward. Out of the corner of my eye, he stared then slowly turned back.

It wasn't long before he pulled into town and into the parking lot of a restaurant. One of the nicer ones in town. The kind that served wine with dinner and had music playing softly in the back. It didn't look like somewhere he would've picked.

I stepped out and wait on Kayce to meet me on the other side of the truck. He gently put his hand on my back, "Is this okay?" He asked.

"Yeah, of course." I smiled and walked with him to the door. He dropped his hand from my back. My skin burned where he had touched and I wished he would do it again.

He once again held the door for me and we stepped in. Immediately Kayce's demeanor changed. He stared off into a corner but I didn't know who or what he was looking at. The hostess gestured for us to follow her but Kayce was zoned out.

I reached out and touched his arm, "Kayce." I said softly.

"Yeah, sorry." He cleared his throat and looked down at me.

"Are you okay?" I asked.

He gave me a small smile. One that made me melt. "Everything's fine. Go ahead, hun."

Hun. It made me giggle a little. Which made him smile bigger. His hand softly touched my back again and gestured me forward. I did so and followed the hostess to a table.

It wasn't long after we sat down someone started walking our way. Kayce stood up. My breath hitched and I expected the worst.

"Kayce, how are you?" The older man stuck his hand out.

Kayce reached out to shake it. "Good. Yourself? How's the hay looking?"

I let out my breath slowly. You have got to calm down, Ada. He's not a monster. Just a man from a small town.

"Well... honestly, not good. If you'll be in office tomorrow I'll swing by." The man looked worried.

"No, I won't be but I'll stop by your place tomorrow morning. No sense for you to run into town anyway." Kayce put his hands in his pockets. I looked up at him, he looked confident. And it looked amazing on him.

"I appreciate it. I'm sorry to intrude, Miss...?" The man smiled at me and waited for me to finish.

"AdaJane. I work with Dr. Stone now." I smiled back at him, adding the part about Dr. Stone so he would hear something familiar.

"A vet. Smart and beautiful. Lucky man, Kayce." He patted Kayce's arm. Kayce chuckled and dropped his head. Something I noticed him doing often when he didn't have any words. I giggled, something I had been doing very often this evening. "Well, you two have a good evening. Tell your dad I said hi for me." And he started to step away.

"Yes sir. You too." Kayce sat down. "I'm sorry." He chuckled.

"It's okay." I smiled. I enjoyed listening to him talk to someone that seemed to respect him so much when I all I ever heard was how people didn't like him. How couldn't you.

"AdaJane, huh?" He teased. "You didn't introduce yourself to me that way."

I rolled my eyes with a smile,"Because I only go by Ada. It slipped."

His smile slowly faded. I noticed him glancing to the corner again during our conversations. And not even ten minutes later I realized why. Three men walked in the door, I had my back turned to it so I didn't even notice until I heard the hostess.

"Can I help you? Sir? You have to have reservations." I glanced over their way.

"Goddammit." Kayce mumbled.

"What? What's wrong?" I looked back to him.

"Just a second. I'm sorry." He pursed his lips together and stood up, starting to walk their way. He stepped outside. I was watching as another man stood up from the corner and walked out. And another walked in behind him. He looked directly at me. And walked my way.

"Sir, you need a reservation." The hostess said once again.

"That's fine. I'll take this one." The man sat in front of me. I wanted to yell for Kayce but I didn't wanna cause a scene.

The hostess started in,"It's fine." I cut her off with a quick response and a smile, hoping the less conflict the better in whatever situation Kayce was in.

The hostess was confused but walked away.

"He's trained you well." The man in front of me chuckled with a smirk under his unkept beard and mustache. The cowboy hat he wore was too big and just looked bad on him. The comment boiled my blood. Trained me? Nasty. I stared at him. Praying Kayce would come in soon. "I bet he hasn't even had time yet. You're fresh bait." He asked, reaching over to my side of the table and grabbing my glass of red wine. He brought it to his lips and gulped some of it down. Fresh bait. You have got to be kidding. I bit my tongue. Just don't say anything to him. "What's wrong, Ada? Don't have anything to say?" My heart raced as he said my name. Who the fuck is this?

"I don't talk to men who can't groom themselves properly." I let the words slip out of my mouth. So much for not saying anything.

He chuckled,"Hmmm. Another spit fire. Seems to be his type. You're just..." he finished the wine and sat the glass back down,"More of my type than his previous choices."

Chills ran down my spine.

"Come on." A voice whispered quietly and I felt someone place a hand on my shoulder. I jumped and looked up. Kayce. I stood up immediately and grabbed his hand. He held tightly to it and started walking out. I glanced back at the man, he winked. I walked closer to Kayce as we stepped outside.

"Wait." I stopped halfway to the truck.

"What?" He turned around, with a panic in his eyes.

"I didn't pay for the wine." I turned around to go back.

"Ada. Fuck the wine, we gotta go, darling." He gently grabbed my arm and started walking me towards the truck. He quickly opened my door and let me in, then did the same on his side. He drove out of the parking lot fast, and down the highway.

I was quiet. I didn't know what happened. And I really didn't want to know. Soon he pulled onto a road that looked familiar. And into a driveway I remembered. The ranch. His ranch.

He pulled up to a huge cabin and put the truck in park. He jumped out. I sat there. Aimlessly staring out the windows and looking at the gorgeous view. Soon the truck door opened,"Ya coming?" He asked.

I unbuckled my seat belt. "Sure." I jumped out of the truck and followed him to the house.

"This isn't fine dining, but I'm not gonna let you go hungry." He stopped on the porch and lit the grill. I smiled, realizing what was happening. He turned around and saw me smiling. "I feel like all I've done to apologize to you since the moment I met you." He let out a deep breath.

I nodded, trying to reassure him,"You have. But it's okay."

"How are you so..." His sentenced trailed off. What was he asking? So clueless? Naïve? Careless? I prepared for the worst. "So calm. And...and just... heavenly."

"Heavenly?" I laughed.

He chuckled and shook his head,"I know. But you... most people that talk to that man are terrified of him. And you were gonna go back inside and pay for the wine you drank." He started laughing.

A smile stayed on my face and felt like it would never leave,"It was rude to leave it!"

"A bunch of criminals interrupted your dinner and you don't even care." He chuckled.

"I don't think that makes me heavenly, Kayce." I teased and leaned up against the porch railings. His face looked calm and relax. Maybe even blissful.

"You're wrong. I've already put you through hell and you just smile through it." He shook his head slowly.

"Well. It wasn't really my kind of date anyway." I shrugged. "This seems better." I quietly spoke, realizing I didn't feel awkward around him anymore. I was comfortable.

"We'll see. We may have to order pizza." He teased and walked into the house. I followed him, still smiling.

*3*

--------------------------------------------------------------

We finished dinner and I stood up to put our plates in the sink, when I noticed my feet hurting from the sandals. I gently put the plates in the sink. Kayces phone rang.

"This should just take a second." He stood up and answered the phone.

"You're fine." I nodded. It gave me a chance to take these damn shoes off. I untied the straps and slipped them off, stretching my toes and feet. I sat them by the front door on an old, Navajo looking rug. The cold wooden floor, chilled me. I walked over to the fire place mantle and looked around. For pictures or something. But nothing. As if no one lived here, nothing personal. I got nosey and looked out the window. The Montana view was picture perfect. The sun had just set and the sky was a summer dream. Oranges and pinks and even some purple clouds complimented the blue mountains. Today was a hotter day and you could tell by the colors that were portrayed. It looked like a postcard.

"The views better from the porch." Kayce raspy voice grumbled quietly from behind me.

I looked over my shoulder at him and smiled. "I'm sure it's even better with a beer."

He let out a little huff,"You're right." He opened the fridge and pulled out a few bottles. He popped open the top of mine then handed it to me, another small gesture that melted my heart. I followed him onto the porch, the warm wind felt nice, dry and not humid like Texas. He leaned against the railing but I chose to sit on the porch swing. One of my favorite things.

"Who was that man earlier?" I asked

"Elliot Whittaker. Used to let me and my brothers fish in his pond when we were kids." He smiled over at me.

"What about the other guys?" I hesitantly asked.

He took a long drink. "Cattle thieves. They steal 'em and run em down to Oklahoma and sell for big money."

I nodded,"So they just don't like you because you're livestock commissioner?" I sipped my beer then pulled my knees to my chest.

He looked over at me. Then he walked to me. And sat down by me. "Do you want the real answer?" He asked. His eyes looked deep into me. I didn't. I really didn't. Just say yeah, that's the problem. That's all it is. Just a simple problem. But I nodded. He sighed, a somber look on his face. "Last year they stole a hundred head of cattle from a neighbor out here. We caught them as they were driving down the road, the cattle all loaded in trailers and shit. Flipped on the sirens to pull them over and they wouldn't. His brother, the one that talked to you, Jake Turner, his brother, James, was driving. And drove off one of the cliffs. Trailer, semi, cattle and all." He leaned forward, resting his elbows on his knees. "Killed everything. Cattle and him both. It was a mess." He wiped his face then finished his beer. He tossed it into bucket by the door. It landed in with a loud clank.

"That's not your fault." I said, confused.

"Well, we knew they were picking up another load later that night." He cleared his throat,"So we pulled James's body out and hung it out by the ranch they were heading to. They got the message. They quit stealing cattle from us out here, just causing other problems now." My jaw nearly dropped. I couldn't get the image of a body hanging out of my head. Your brothers body hanging. And seeing that. He looked back at me then stood up."You want me to take you home now?" He asked. I thought hard for a second. About what he just told me. Trying to process it. He did it help everyone. He just said they stopped stealing the cattle. It was a validated reason. Not a very good one. But it was to protect his neighbors. His people. "It's okay if you want too. You've made it longer than most do. Most stop whenever they hear the stories." He leaned down and rested his arms on the railing.

"Kayce," I got up and stood beside him,"I've heard a lot about you. But I won't believe any of it until I hear it from you." I reached out and rested my hand on his forearm. He stared straight into the night and I thought maybe I lost him again.

"You want another beer?" He tilted his head.

I didn't lose him. I smiled. "If you drink one with me."

"That's one thing I can do." He reached over and patted my hand that was resting on his arm. He stood up straight and walked back into the cabin. I followed him inside. He pulled out another drink, opened it, and handed it to me. I hopped up onto the counter and sipped on it. He stood in front of me, leaning against the kitchen island, staring and drinking his beer.

Within minutes, I heard foot steps on the porch. I could see Kayce listening for who it was. I was nervous at first but then I heard laughing and the screen door open.

"Wake up ya piece of shit, we're going bar hopping!" A strong accent rang out. I exploded into a fit of laughter, shaking my head.

"I'm awake, Rip." Kayce called out, chuckling.

The cowboy turned the corner, beer in hand, and cowboy hat on his head. His beard was scruffy and he had large shoulders and a broad chest. Did they only have good looking men working here? Rip froze when he saw me.

"Oh fuck." His eyes widened and he looked from me to Kayce back to me,"Ma'am. Sorry." He nodded at me.

I contained my laughter,"Well when are we leaving?" I asked.

Kayce looked over at me and Rip started chuckling. He smacked Kayce on the back then pointed at me,"Come on, girl. We're going now."

And out the door he went. Kayce shook his head at me, smiling from ear to ear. "You're gonna be trouble around here, I can feel it."

I jumped off the counter and down the rest of my beer then tossed it in the trash. "I heard you were into trouble." I teased and slipped in my painful sandals on.

"Yes ma'am." He smirked.

We walked outside. The truck was piled up with guys. The only room left was in the back seat. Only one seat.

Kayce opened the truck door for me. All the guys stopped talking and laughing. They stared.

"Who the fuck is this?" A black cowboy in corner asked.

"This is Ada. Careful, she bites." Kayce said with a serious face.

They all stared. I felt awkward for a minute. Unwanted and overstepping.

"How do you find these women?" The man next to him threw his hands in the air. "We live on a ranch, a  sausage party if you will, and you always come up with something like that."

"Ryan, you better watch it. Last time you hit on his woman you were spitting up dirt for a week." Someone from the front seat called back.

"Jimmy, shut the fuck up." Ryan called back.

"And he didn't even like that one." An older, Sam Elliot look alike, with a raspy voice hollered from the front seat. I chuckled and stepped up into the truck.

"You're not wrong." Kayce squeezed in beside me, draping his arm behind my shoulders. Now there were four of us in the back seat. "Ryan, I wanna see your hands the whole fucking time." Kayce growled. There were some Oh's and Oo's from the other cowboys, knowing it was a joke. But I looked up at Kayce, with a small smile. He winked at me and I leaned into him a little more. He squeezed my shoulder and somehow managed to pull me closer. He was warm. I could've fell into him and stayed there like that all night.

The first bar we pulled into was crowded. We stayed for a few minutes but the guys didn't like someone that was there so I convinced them to leave instead of starting a brawl. The next bar was still busy but not as rowdy.

"You need a beer?" Lloyd asked me as he down next to me at the bar.

I lightly shook my beer, it felt light. "Yeah, if you're offering." I spun my chair around to face the bar. I had been busy watching Kayce and Rip annihilate Ryan and Jimmy at pool.

The bartender brought us one more each.

"You don't look like you belong with someone like Kayce." He took a swig of his beer.

I nodded slowly. "That's what I've been told." I spun my chair back to watch the boys. I smiled as Rip made their last shot. Ryan started in about how Kayce and Rip took the better pool sticks and that's how they won.

"Be careful around here." He grumbled.

I looked at him, a little pissed off. This man had no business telling me what to do or who I can be around. "Ive been told that too." I smarted back a little.

He took a swig out of his beer. "Apparently not enough."

My blood boiled for some reason. I clenched my jaw. "I'm sorry, is there a problem or are you just normally an ass?"

He snapped his head towards me. "I'm trying to watch out for you."

"You don't even know me." I fired back. "And I don't need anyone watching out for me. I appreciate the gesture but please. Leave it alone. I know what I'm getting into." I stood up to go somewhere else. Anywhere else.

I was wrong. I had no idea idea what I was getting into but I didn't need some old man griping at me about it either.

Kayce was smiling as he looked over and met my eyes. He gestured me to come to him.

"Yes?" I asked, taking a sip of my new beer.

"Everything okay?" He leaned around me, looking at Lloyd.

I leaned with him, tilting my head to obstruct his view. "Everything's fine, Kayce." I smiled. I didn't wanna cause problems between them. Not this soon. He narrowed his eyes and looked above me instead of around me.

He didn't believe me and that's fine. But this isn't happening. Not here. "Hey," I reached up and tilted his chin back down to look me in the eyes. "I'm just here to have fun. Don't worry about it." I gave him a sweet smile and batted my eyes.

I saw his mood change, maybe even a blush. "You know how to play?" He nodded to the table. The boys walked over to get more drinks. I laughed and my face turned red. I knew what was coming. I shook my head at him. "Come on. I'll show you how." I rolled my eyes playfully and took the stick from him. He stood behind me and put his hand on my right elbow. "Loosen up some." I did so. He grabbed my left hand and sat it on the table, slightly bending me over. "Rest it between...here." He positioned the stick between my two knuckles. "Thats how you aim. If you bend down a little more, you can look down the stick and line it up your shot."

I bent down more. My ass now pushing against him, "Like that?" I whispered.

He moved his hand to my hip, "Mhmm. Perfect." He leaned over and grabbed a ball to line it up with the cue ball. "Now pull back." I moved my right arm back. "And hit the ball, "He leaned over my shoulder, his face close to mine. He touched the center of the white, cue ball. "Right there."

I looked at him. "How many times have you done this?" I whispered.

"Played pool?" He furrowed his eyebrows beneath his hat.

I shook my head, "No. How many times have you pulled this stunt with a girl?"

He nodded a little, "Too many."

I stood up and stared at him. "If that's what you want out of this, just let me know."

"Want what?" He was confused.

I sighed,"If all you want is a hook up, that's fine-"

His eyes widened a little and he cut me off,"No, no. Not at all. That's not what I'm after. Well," He swallowed. "I'm not gonna lie and say I ain't been thinking bout it but tonight's not the time for that."

I giggled a little, but was still not sure what to think. "Promise?" I asked.

"I promise." He pushed my hair being my ear. I smiled then leaned down and shot the ball into the pocket.

"Beginners luck."

"No," I chuckled. "Years of practice." I handed the stick back.

I almost watched his jaw unhinge. "What?"

I gulped some of my beer then wiped my mouth,"Kayce, I'm from Texas. It's illegal to not know how to play pool, line dance, or lasso."

He scoffed,"I'll be damned." He gave me the stick back,"Then you wouldn't mind losing a few games."

A grin built on my face,"I wouldn't mind winning a few, no."

**4**

- - - - - - - - - - - - - - - - - - - - - - - - - - - - - - - - - - - - - - - - - - - - - - - -

Within the hour, I had won 3 games and he had won 2. I was little rusty. I had plenty of beer in me and whiskey was my next option. It was Friday, I didn't have to work tomorrow unless I was called in, which rarely happened.

I sipped on a few Maker and Diets while the rest of them got into a pissing match of taking shots.

"Y'all better wrap it up, we gotta work tomorrow." Lloyd stood up from the bar. Colby started to stand up but wobbly sat back down.

"In a minute." He said.

I chuckled at his clumsy and drunkness. I felt a hand come from behind me and rest on my hip. I looked back over my shoulder and saw Kayce looking down, smirking at me. I leaned back into him a little.

We all made our way back to the truck to head back. Instead of squeezing four across, I made myself comfortable on Kayces lap.

They dropped us off at the cabin and then headed down the hill. We made it inside the door. I took my shoes off, stumbling slightly. My feet were killing. Kayce leaned against the kitchen counter, watching me.

"Can I help you?" I giggled.

He shrugged,"Just looking."

"At?" I walked up to him slowly.

"The most beautiful thing I've ever seen." He said quietly with a serious face. I reached out and smoothed down the denim shirt on his chest. He looked down at me. No smile or smirk or anything. Just the deep brown eyes melting into mine. I blinked slowly up at him. "If you keep looking at me like that, I'm might have to break that promise."

I smiled. "Sorry." I took a step back. "Guess I'm kinda asking for it." I made the comment before I even realized what I said out loud.

He stood up straighter. "No. The only time you're asking for it is if you ask me for it. You understand?" His eyes were full of concern and worry. I nodded. "I don't want you to feel like that. Or think like that. Not here." He shook his head slowly. "Not with me."He released a breath.

It only made me want him more. But this is only the third time I've seen him. It's too soon. I barely know him. I kept trying to tell himself.

I stepped back up to him and pressed my lips to his cheek. "Thank you."

He smiled a little and again, it was contagious. "I guess I better take you home before Hannah sends out the sheriff."

I giggled and agreed with him. The drive back was quiet but peaceful. He pulled up in front of the clinic. "I'll walk you up." He unbuckled his seat belt.

"It's okay. I'll make it." I unbuckled mine as well. He nodded.

"I don't even have your number." He spoke up as I opened the door.

"You know where to find me if you need me." I winked at him and jumped out of the truck.

He chuckled,"Alright... goodnight, Ada."

"Good night." I closed the truck door and made my way inside and upstairs.

I pushed open the door and made my way in.

"About time." Hannah was watching a movie in the living room, I was surprised she was awake.

I giggled,"Hannah... it was..." I had no words. I closed the door behind me and leaned against it.

"Was what?" She laughed.

I sighed and flopped onto the couch beside her. "I don't know. He's so... Just kind. And... and thoughtful. Just caring and kind and thoughtful." I shook my head and closed my eyes, remembering how he looked at me. Those eyes.

She chuckled,"Girl you've got it bad." She tossed a handful of popcorn into her mouth.

"What?" I turned my head to look at her.

"You're in love."

"No!" Was I? No. "No!" I yelled again. "I'm not in love. It's too soon. He's just a good guy. That's all." I stood up to go take a shower.

"But he's not, Ada." Hannah said sadly. I turned around and looked at her, with knowing eyes. Even Kayce himself told me so. He's not.

"I know." I whispered.

*****

I woke up the next morning with a headache and dry mouth. I trudged to the bathroom and brushed my teeth for a long amount of time, mostly still asleep. Then I zombie walked into the kitchen and popped a few ibuprofen in my mouth and chugged down an orange Gatorade.

"How do you feel?" Hannah chuckled as she sat at the counter and ate an eggo waffle.

I groaned,"Not great. I'm out of practice for this lifestyle." I rubbed my eyes.

"You're gonna be ecstatic to know that you've gotta a case then." She shoved nearly a quarter of the waffle in her mouth.

You've gotta be fucking kidding me. The one time I go out.

"Okay." I nodded and opened the ibuprofen bottle back up, tossing a few more in then hurried to my bed room and pulled on a pair of navy blue scrubs. I tied my hair back into bun and pulled the head wrap up around my ears and past my forehead. "Text me the address!" I hollered at Hannah as I ran out the door, apple in hand and a few more gatorades. I stopped in my tracks and went back inside, grabbing the bottle of ibuprofen and tucked in of my scrub pockets. I'm sure I'll need it.

"Yeah, Ada's already headed there now. Why? Oh god. Okay." I heard Hannah on the phone in the other room.

"What's going on?" I called out to her.

"They'll catch you up when you get there. Hurry!" Hannah yelled back.

I ran out the door and quickly down the stairs, nearly missing some. I checked my phone and pulled up the address. I floored it there, driving like a bat outta hell. I didn't know what was going on but if Hannah was panicking it had to be bad. I pulled up to the place in less than ten minutes. I jumped out of the truck and looked for anyone.

A man rode up over the hill on a horse. It was Elliot Whittaker, the man Kayce spoke to last night. I ran his way.

"AdaJane. Nice to see you again. Let me take you to them." He reached his hand down from his horse.

"Mr. Whittaker," I nodded and grabbed his hand, and jumped, pulling myself onto the horses back. I held onto him as he sped up. When we broke over the hill, I saw multiple men at the bottom, by a pond. Mostly likely the pond Kayce mentioned. As we rode closer, I could see they were all surrounding a ring of stock panels, there were four cattle in the fencing and one laying down on the outside. It looked dead.I jumped off before Mr. Whittaker even stopped. Jogging up to the men and the dead cow. "Whats going on?" I asked.

A cowboy from inside the ring looked over my way. I made eye contact with him. Kayce. Of course he was here. He told Mr. Whittaker he would stop by. All I wanted was to say hi and be happy but I couldn't. There were bigger problems.

"I came out to check the hay for Elliot," A young guy, maybe even a teenager started to speak up,"And some of the cows were groaning and coughing. We separated 'em and this were the ones we noticed doing it."

Groaning and coughing.

"What about that one?" I gestured to the dead cow.

"Just died about fifteen minutes ago. Just fell over." One of the old cowboys said.

I asked Mr. Whittaker some questions and decided what I had to do. "You gotta head restraint?" I asked. He shook his head. Damn. This is gonna be a shit show. "Alright. Kayce, you may wanna get out." I stepped up onto the panels and slung my leg over.

"I'll be fine." He mumbled.

"Suit yourself." I brushed off my hands and slowly walked up to one of the girls. I scratched her head, then up to her ears. "They seem pretty tame." I spoke up to Mr. Whittaker.

"Thank you. I work with 'em a lot." He said with a prideful voice.

"You can tell." I nodded and gently ran my hand to its back. I lightly pressed on it back, then grasped a little harder.

The cow groaned loudly and took off in a bolt. Kayce scrambled up the fence a few steps and I did the same. "I see why you wanted a head lock." He said with a breathy voice.

"Yeah." I wiped the dust from my eyes. "They've got what Dr. Stone would call Hardware Disease. Causes tears and perforations to the reticulum. By the looks of it, I'd say that one," I pointed over to the dead one,"Had it, and all those tears got infected." I sat on top of the gate and swung my legs over to the other side, talking out to Mr. Whittaker.

"Hardware Disease?" Kayce questioned. "Like swallowing metal?"

I nodded,"Basically. Have these other ones being coughing, vomiting, anything like that?" Mr. Whittaker shook his head, along with the other boys. "Good. Easy fix. All I have to do drop a magnet into there reticulum. We'll treat with some antibiotics just incase they are infected, maybe we can catch it before they die of it. Okay with you?" I asked Mr. Whittaker.

He furrowed his eyebrows. "Thats fine. But I don't have any metal out here." He shook his head.

"Have you drove through your pastures recently? For beef cattle like this, it's normally barb wire fencing or the wires from steel belted tires." He shook his head again. I pressed my lips together. "I can run an ultrasound and see what's in there. I have no problem doing that. But..." I sighed. "Unfortunately, it's extremely expensive. I will gladly do it, but I think it's not necessary. I have no doubt in my mind, that's what your cattle have."

He stared at me, then looked at Kayce. Then back at me. "You're a good vet. I trust you. Just do the magnets and antibiotics." He nodded.

"I'm gonna sedate them. There's no way I can run a balling gun down their throat without a head restraint." I jumped off the fence and dug through my bag, grabbing everything I needed. I stood up to go back over, but stopped. The dead cow laid there in front of me. "Mr. Whittaker?" I asked.

"Please, call me Elliot." He walked up to me.

I smiled,"I wouldn't mind to pump that cows reticulum. Maybe we can see what it's ingested."

He nodded,"Yeah, that would helpful. Thank you."

I sedated all four cows and got to work dropping in magnets. By the time I was finished, my arms sore and I was sweating up a storm. It only took a couple hours. I jumped back over the fence and grabbed my pump as I saw someone ride over the hill. Kayce was back.

"Hey." I wiped the sweat from my forehead.

"Hey." He dismounted his horse. "You want some help?"

I chuckled,"If you've got a strong stomach."

He grinned,"I think I'll be fine." He squatted down and position the cows mouth open for me.

I worked the pumps hose down the throat and into the reticulum and started pumping. The smell was terrible, as usual.

"Whoa." Kayce coughed and stepped back.

My stomach turned and I keep pumping out the fluid. Sooner, little shiny pieces were floating in the phlegm.

"What is that?" I asked, looking closer. Kayce squatted down, covering his nose with his shirt.

"Roofing nails." He shook his head.

"Why would he have roofing nails in his field?" I shook the excess phlegm off the tubing and packed up my bag.

Kayce stood up and sighed. "I don't know. But a bunch of equipment and supplies were stole from the barn we were building few weeks ago."

"From your barn?" I wiped the sweat from my upper lip with my forearm.

He nodded slowly.

Another Kayce related problem.

5

------------------------------------------------------------

I tried to stay engulfed in my work. We were busy and Dr. Stone wasn't at the office as much. I was the only other one who cared for livestock. Everyone else was house pets and small animals. I woke up early and went out on calls then didn't get back until dark. Dr. Stone gave me the on call cell phone now. No more relaying calls, it went straight to me.

Around 5am the phone rang. I groaned and sat up quickly. Then cleared my throat to not sound so dead. "It's Ada."

"Ada, hey. Sorry, I thought I called Dr. Stone." It was a familiar voice. Kayce.

"You did but he's out today. Whatcha need?" I rubbed my eyes and yawned, already losing my patience for the day.

"I've got new horses coming in today. I was needing him to look over them before we kept 'em." He also had no patience today either.

"Yeah. I'll be there. What time are they being dropped off?" I stood up out of bed and started to change, expecting for Kayce to tell me they were already there.

There was silence on the other end of the line. "I don't mean anything by this, but it really needs to be Dr. Stone who checks them out."

I froze. Are you fucking kidding, is what I wanted to say. But instead I sighed. "I understand. But he's not available." I chewed on my lip. Please don't ask any questions.

"Ada, you don't understand-"

"I do. This is my job and I know what I'm doing." I said sternly. Kayce is not a crush, he is a client. And I know my work better than him. "Once again, Dr. Stone isn't available today. I would be more than happy to check them out. I just need to know a time so I can make arrangements. Now is this going to work out or are you still going to treat me like I'm incapable?" This was a confidence I only had when it came to work. I would've never spoke up before this way.

"It's fine. They're already here. Thanks." And then the line dropped.

I sighed and shook my head. This is gonna be a mess.

I jumped into whatever clean scrubs I could find and made my way to the ranch, dreading ever second and regretting what I had told to Kayce. It was rude and unprofessional. When I pulled up, there was a small trailer. A dingy looking one. Not what I was expecting. I jumped out of the truck and walked towards Kayce. I also started regretting not bringing a jacket, it was cold this morning.

"Morning." He nodded at me, barely even looking my way as he opened the gate on the horse trailer.

"Good morning." It came out as a small voice. I stepped over to look inside. I immediately realized why he didn't want me here. I nodded and sighed. I looked around, but didn't see a driver. I assumed he didn't want me to see him. "What the hell, Kayce?"

He dropped his head. "We do it all the time."

"You steal horses from other people?" I rested my hands on my hips. I stared at the brand on the boney hip that looked nothing like a Yellowstone brand.

"I don't want you involved. It's not that I thought you couldn't do it. I just didn't want you too." His eyes looked sad and tired. They were a little red too. Maybe he was sick. Or just tired.

"Why'd you take them?" I asked quietly.

"About to starve to death. Neighbor says the owner beats 'em. Figured we can break and take care of 'em here." He spoke lowly and softly. This morning voice he had was extremely sexy. It was raspy and deep.

Stay focused.

"Alright," I rubbed my face,"You want a copy of immunizations, owner-ship paperwork, anything else?"

"You don't have to do this." He shook his head.

"Would Dr. Stone?" I asked. The look he gave me said yes. "Then yeah. I do. I'll have it ready by tomorrow. Let's treat them with some antibiotics too. No telling what they're sick with. And keep them isolated from until they start putting on weight. I wanna make sure they don't have any parasites that can be contagious-"

He cut me off. "I need them soon."

I shot back at him almost before he could even finish the sentence. "We do this my way." I swallowed hard, not wanting to argue with him. Not wanting to stand up against him but this is my career. And I know what's best for those horses. I had to keep telling myself this. Stay strong. "I don't care how Dr. Stone did it. This is how I'm doing it. If they're contagious," I pointed to the trailer then out to his barns,"Then they're all dead. And I'm not gonna be responsible for you losing 2 million dollars worth of horses." I let out a deep breath.

He stared into my eyes. Thinking. He's either pissed or respects me. I just couldn't tell which one it was. "Yes ma'am." He nodded and started to walk away.

"Kayce..." I said with a different tone now.

"They'll be isolated." He nodded again. "We'll do it your way." He mumbled.

"I was just going to say it was nice to see you again." A smile crept up on my face. This is terrible timing. What the hell are you doing.

"Yeah," His eyed me up and down,"You too."

"Who the fuck is this?" I heard someone from behind me holler.

I turned to see an older man stomping our way. "I'm Dr. Stones tech, Ada." I helped my hand out.

He stared at my hand then looked at Kayce. "What the fuck are you thinking?" I dropped my hand then looked at Kayce myself.

"Dad, I trust her." He blinked slowly.

Dad. Okay, makes sense. Trust me? I'll be damned. You were just arguing with me.

The man stared at me. John Dutton stared at me. "John." He stuck his hand out.

I looked at it for a second then shook his hand. "Ada." I said hesitantly.

"I hope you understand-" he started in.

"I understand everything. It was nice meeting you, but I have to get back to work." I nodded to him, then glanced back at Kayce. "I'll drop the papers and antibiotics off tomorrow. I don't want you to be seen at the clinic, just in case."

"Alright."

And I stomped off to my truck.

*****

The cool morning faded into an extremely hot day. Even for me. Even my Texas skin tanned more somehow. I got home late that night and couldn't wait to get a shower. Hannah wasn't going to be home tonight. She was with her dad. He had a doctors appointment today. A serious one.

I pulled out my phone and swiped through to find her name. I put it on speaker then set it on the counter by the fridge as I dug thru to see what I could find to fix.

"Hey." Her voice sounded tired. And sad. I froze.

"Hey. Just checking in. How'd it go?" I already knew the answer.

The other end was silent. Then I heard a sniffle. "It's bad, Ada." Her voice cracked and she sniffled again followed by a cry.

I tried to hold it together but it hurt listening to her cry and knowing I could do nothing about it. "Is it cancer?" My voice sounded weak, like it wasn't even my own voice.

"Pancreas. It's already spread to his liver."

"Pancreas?" I repeated. "That's...but that's rare. Are they sure?"

More sniffles and cries, and then she said,"Positive. They can operate but you know how that goes."

"Surgeries more dangerous than the cancer." I finished her thought. "Damn. I'm sorry, Hannah." I wanted to hug her and see her. My heart ached for her.

What will this town do without him? What are we gonna do with the clinic?

"Hows everything at the clinic?" She asked.

I sighed and pulled some salmon out of the fridge. "It's good. No troubles here. Well, the girls said they had a rabid squirrel in the office earlier, but thankfully, I had bigger fish to fry at the time." I chuckled, trying to lighten the mood.

She gave a little laugh. "Good. I think we're gonna go to the Mount Helena and the cathedral tomorrow and then come home in a couple days. I know you can handle it, but if you need us to come back-"

I cut her off. "No. Spend as much time with him as you needed. I've got everything covered here, Han."

It was silent again. "Thank you."

"Don't thank me. I'm your best friend. That's why I'm here. Give him a big squeeze for me and call if you need anything." I said cheerfully.

"I will," She sniffled again,"I love you, Ada." Her voice cracked again.

My heart shattered. She was hurting so bad. "I love you too. Good night."

"Goodnight." And then she hung up.

I let out a shaky breath. "Okay. It's okay." I tried to not think about Dr. Stone or what would happen. I just ignored it and fixed myself dinner. I tossed the salmon in the oven while I took a quick shower.

I ate dinner and caught up on some episodes of Law and Order. When I started to doze off, my phone rang.

I picked it up, "It's Ada." I tried hard to keep from yawning.

"Hi, is this the emergency vet?" A sweet, woman's vice answered back to me.

"Yes ma'am. What can I do you for?" I sat up and started walking to my room, ready to change clothes.

"Well, my donkey just stomped some coyotes but he's been bitten or scratched and I can't get the bleeding to stop. I'm needing some help." Her old voice was shaky and nervous.

"I'll be out there shortly. What's your address, ma'am?"

*****

The next day I made sure to finish up the paperwork for the new Dutton horses. Once things seemed to settle down at the clinic, I drove out to the ranch.

It was hot again today. The hottest day of the year in Montana. This of course called for a beautiful, summer sun set. The dark orange and red sky reminded me of Texas. I missed it to an extent. I missed my friends and Texas itself. I miss the heat and the beach and the friendly people. Montana was full of people consistently fighting for something. It's a different world here.

Kayce wasn't in any of the barns. It had just gotten dark so I figured he was still working but I didn't see him anywhere. I went to check the bunkhouse, assuming he would be there or at least someone there would know where he is.

I could hear laughing and noise from a ways away. I opened the door and it quieted a little, then completely when everyone looked at me. Jimmy, Ryan, and Colby were at the table, along with others who were playing poker or some kind of card game.

"Ada, hey." Ryan stood up.

I saw Rip in the corner of my eye. He was laying on one of the top bunks with his hat resting over his face. I watched as he jerked the hat off his face and sat up, looking my way. He jumped down from the bed.

"Hey, I was trying to find Kayce. I've got some antibiotics for y'all." I shoved my hands in my pockets as Rip walked towards us.

"I think he's at the house. I'll take ya up there." Rip nodded.

Ryan sat back down, "See ya around."

I smiled and followed Rip back out the door. "I know where his cabin is, I can make it there." I said to him as we were walking.

"I think he's at the main house. It's best that you don't just show up there."

"Oh." I nodded. Weird.

Once again, the way people act here is so strange.

6

-------------------------------------------------------------

R ip knocked on the cabin door. Seconds later, the door flung open.

"What?" Kayce asked hatefully, breathing heavy and hard. He glanced at me quickly.

"She's yours." Rip nodded to me and walked off the porch.

Kayce still looked pissed,"What's going on?" He asked in a hushed voice.

I shook my head and shrugged, holding out the folder with all the paper work he would need for the horses,"Nothing. Just dropping off the paper-work and antibiotics."

"Thanks." He opened the folder, scanning through the pages. "Looks good." He nodded,"Perfect, really."

I ignored the comments. "Antibiotics are in the truck. I didn't know if you wanted to start them tonight or in the morning." Please day in the morning.

He looked up from the paper,"'Mornings fine." Yes. Thank you.

"Alright, I'll leave them in the barn. Just holler if you need something." I turned to walk down the porch.

"Wait-" Kayce stepped out onto the porch with me. "You're already out here, you might as well stay as while." He gave a small smile.

"No, it's okay-" I shook my head.

"I know you're busy and don't have time to come out here." He let out a deep breath and cleared his throat,"But I'd like to take you out again. I had a good time."

"I did too." I smiled a little. I thought back to that night. How excited and happy he made me feel.

"Then stay." He gave me a deep look. On that I couldn't say no too. Not to those eyes.

"Okay." I whispered.

"Come on in." He gestured inside the house and I followed him into a living area. It was gorgeous house. "Lemme talk to dad real quick and then we'll head to my cabin." He took off in a different direction.

I sat down on the couch, nervous. My hands were sweaty and I felt a little awkward. Like a young girl waiting for a boys parents to leave except we were the ones leaving. He came back out moments later. "Ready?"

"Yeah." I hopped up and followed him out.

His cabin was cold. Like he had on the air all day, but now that it cooled off tonight, it was freezing in here. I folded my arms over each other and rubbed them, trying to warm them up a little. "You want a beer?" He asked.

"How about whiskey?" I teased and sat down on his couch.

"Whatever you want." He grabbed a glass whiskey bottle, half full, out of a cabinet. He brought over two small glasses and poured us a drink. He had it to me. I took a sip and it burned my throat but warmed my stomach.

"How you found a new wrangler yet?" I asked him.

He threw back the whiskey and sat the glass down. He wiped his mouth and shook his head. "No. Not yet." I nodded. "How's doc doing?" He asked quietly. He knew. I don't know how, but he knew.

I shrugged and stared at the brown liquid in my cup. I took another sip. "Not good. Hannah's freaking out, and she has every reason too but it's still taking a toll on hear." I sniffled a little. I was worried about Dr. Stone of course, but really worried about Hannah. She was shutting down. Not talking or laughing. Just worrying all the time.

"Pancreas?" He asked. I nodded. "Damn." He poured himself another glass then gestured the bottle to me. I finished off my drink then let him pour him another one. "So you've been running the clinic by yourself?"

"Yeah." I sighed, trying to relax and not seem so tense and nervous. I pulled my legs up and sat cross legged, facing him. It looked like a little smile pulled up on his face. "What?" I asked, smiling now.

He let the smile onto his face and shook his head. He grabbed the whiskey bottle and just took a swig out of it. "You're just..." He poured himself another glass and sat back. "Just something."

I giggled,"What's that suppose to mean?" I took a sip and let it burn my mouth before swallowing.

He opened his mouth to speak but then closed it. "I don't know how the fuck you're running that place. You're the only one there who does cattle."

"I'm the only one who does large animals at all." I shrugged. "I'm just trying to keep it afloat will he's gone. When they come back, I'll have Hannah."

"Hannah doesn't do big animals." He finished off his whiskey again and sat it down.

I did the same, deciding I need to slow down. "Yeah." I nodded. He poured me another glass and another for himself. "When Dr. Stone is back up to health, it won't be so bad." Kayce handed me the glass and gave me a knowing look. We both knew he wouldn't be coming back. Maybe here and there but he wouldn't be coming back to stay. Hannah and I needed to make a plan. But how do you make a plan with someone who's father is dying? "What am I gonna do?" I asked quietly.

He reached out and grabbed my hand, gave it a little squeeze and said, "We'll figure something out. You're not alone."

I felt alone. I felt so lonely. Even with him here, I felt completely on my own. There was no way I could go back to school now. Hannah wouldn't be able to run the clinic on her own. I let it sink in. I wasn't ever going to be a vet. My eyes got a little blurry with tears. From exhaustion, stress, and worry. I sniffled and threw back the rest of the whiskey, and poured myself another glass. "Let's talk about something else." I whispered.

He nodded. "Do you ride horses or just take care of 'em?" He threw his arm up on the top of the couch. He was more open to me now. It felt welcoming and inviting. Just this small movement made me want to fall into the gap between his arm and chest. To lay there and close my eyes, slowing fall asleep to sound of him breathing and the smell of his clothing.

I grinned, "I ride. Just haven't in a long time."

"did y'all have cattle?" He took the cowboy hat off his head and tossed it on the table. He was even more comfortable with me now. It was the first time I had seen him without a hat and I wasn't disappointed.

He ran a hand through his hair and I realized how long it was. I never liked the looks of long hair on men, that was until now.

I picked up my glass,"We were too broke to have cattle," I took a sip then set it back down,"Rodeos and rode wherever we could."

A smirk grew on his face,"What, were you a barrel racer or sum'thin?"

I threw my head back laughing,"I bet you wish I was a barrel racer." When I look back at him I started to feel the affects of the whiskey. It seemed as if my eyes couldn't catch up with my movements.

He threw his hands up,"Just asking." He grinned.

I shook my head, smiling ear to ear. "Steer wrestling and team roping."

"Alright, not what I would've guessed." He chuckled and stood up.

I watched as he walked to the fridge and pulled out a beer. I folded my arms on top of the couch, and rested my chin on them. Feeling flirty, I watched him carefully. He walked with a confidence I hadn't ever since on anyone in my entire life. He was sure of himself but not overly conceited. He was comfortable to talk about horses and cattle and Montana, but anything else, it was as if his personality was gone. Maybe that was a Navy Seal thing. Or just a military thing. Maybe I could break him of it. I wanted him to be comfortable and worry free around me.

He glanced over at me, and then back again, surprised to see me watching him. "You want one?" He nodded to the bottle.

"Yeah." I bit my lip and nodded. He kept eye contact with me as he grabbed another from the fridge and strolled over to me. He popped it open and went to hand it to me. "I don't want that one." I said with a serious face, teasing.

"Well," He looked confused,"What do you want?"

"That one." I reached for the beer in his other hand.

A small chuckle escaped his lips and he let me have it. "Whatever you want, darling." He turned back to the kitchen and tossed the bottle tabs in the trash bin.

Darling. There's that word again.

I took a swig from the beer. It was nice and cold on my throat. It felt especially nice after the hot, burning whiskey.

Kayce flipped the switch on an old radio. The Texas country music floated through the air. He leaned against the wall next to it. "You've got good taste." I nodded.

"Yeah." He let out a short breath and drank his beer.

"The musics good too." I winked.

He looked confused again but then caught on. "Good taste in women huh?"

"So I've heard." I sat the beer on the table because my empty whiskey glass and the near empty bottle.

He nodded slowly. "I don't know. Ain't worked out to well yet." He mumbled while looking at the dark bottle.

I stood up slowly. "I think you're on the right path." I walked up to him, feeling brave.

"Yeah?" He asked.

I nodded, grabbing the beer from his hand and setting it on the table beside mine. "Yeah." Then I replaced my hand where the bottle was. "Do you know how to dance?" I asked softly.

"No, but I can try." He reached out and snaked his arm around my waist. His touch set me on fire. I giggled as he pulled me closer to him.

He wasn't wrong. He couldn't dance. But he tried. "You're terrible." I laughed, trying to help him.

He slowly stopped, just smiling and staring down at me. "Yeah, but it made you laugh." He let go of my hand and brought it to my face. I rested my hands on his chest, looking up into his caring eyes. The callouses felt rough on my cheek, especially when he rubbed it with his thumb.

"Is that your excuse?" I whispered.

He nodded and leaned down a little. "Okay?"

Of course it was okay. I had been thinking about it since I first met him. I wanted to know how soft his lips were. You never know if you truly love someone until you share the moment when there's no space between you. "Yeah." I whispered and closed my eyes as our lips met.

Yes.

I melted into his chest as he held me tight to him. I pushed my lips into him. I wanted to be as close as possible. This is what it feels like. This is that feeling they tell you about your whole life. Your heart racing and hands shaking. This is how it's suppose to be. This is what was meant to be. This is why I came to Montana and met Hannah at vet school and ever decided to go to vet school in the first place. To end up here. With him.

He pulled as softly, then kissed me again, but this time with more passionate. I opened my mouth slightly and kissed back, fighting for control but it wasn't up to me. His tongue skimmed my bottom lip and I couldn't help but let out a small moan, maybe even a whimper.

"Don't do that." He mumbled against my lips. I closed the gap between again. It was my turn. Our tongues met softly just before this kiss ended.

"Why?" I mumbled back, kissing him once more.

"Cause I don't fuck on the second date." His kiss was more aggressive this time.

Him saying that was enough to satisfying any need I had in the moment. "This is not a date." I teased, pulling back, smiling. He shook his head but leaned back in. And we continued to kiss for what could've been hours but felt like a brief time.

He stopped slowly. I tried to open my eyes. My eyes felt heavy. Very heavy. And I felt lightheaded. My eyes. They felt half open. Pull yourself together.

"You feeling okay?" He asked.

I nodded with a little grin, "Yeah, just too much whiskey." I giggled a little.

"Alright." He chuckled. The laugh was short but joyful. I wished I could make him laugh again but I couldn't think of anything funny to say. He pecked my lips again. "Think you might wanna lay down? I think I'm just holding you up at this point."

I tried to get a grip but still couldn't. I was past that point. "Good idea." I blinked slowly as he walked me somewhere. I didn't know where but soon he took me in a dark room. And it was cold. He let go of me briefly and I swayed a little. Then he picked me up. "Whoa." I dropped my head onto his shoulder. It made me dizzy and nauseous.

Fuck, Ada. Do not throw up on this man. Don't throw up at all.

Then he sat me down into a bed. And pulled a blanket up over me. "Holler if you need something." He kissed my forehead softly.

"Where are you going?" I asked, slurring a little more than I expected.

"Not far away. I'll be right in here. Good night, Ada."

I smiled. "Night." And I rolled over, inhaling deeply. It smelled like home and safety and comfort.

7

------------------------------------------------------------

Water. I need water.

I opened my eyes and blinked a couple times. The room was freezing and dark. Nothing like the loft. I'm at Kayces still.

Fuck, I'm at Kayce's.

I scrambled, looking for my work cell. I scooped it up off the nightstand. No missed calls. I sighed, relieved.

My head ached a little so I rubbed my eyes and stood up. I was a little wobbly on my feet as always the next morning after I drank.

"Why the fuck are you sleeping on the couch?" I heard a females voice in another room. My heart dropped and raced at the same time. Who is this? I thought him and Monica were divorced. Is that Monica?

Oh, god. Oh, what do I do? I sat back down on the bed and tried to listen, but couldn't hear anything that Kayce was saying, if anything at all.

"Like the vet?" The female voice said again. Must not be Monica. Surely he wouldn't just tell her I was in here. Who is this then? Doesn't he have a sister? Maybe it's her.

I sighed and decided it didn't matter who it was. If they didn't like I was here, they would have to fight me in the shower because that's where I'm headed. I flipped on the light to his bathroom and looked around. Not bad. Not as bad as I thought anyway. Just a pair of dirty jeans in the floor and... oh God, no hand soap. Jesus.

I turned on the shower and stripped off my clothes. I let the water soak into me. I close my eyes and enjoyed it. It was peaceful here. Something about the whole place relaxed me and made me feel comfortable.

I was interrupted when the door opened. I almost froze, remembering the door was glass, but realized it didn't matter. He knew what his bathroom looked like and he can hear the shower running so if he chooses to open that door then he knows what's coming.

"Do you drink coffee?" He asked.

I slid open the door and leaned out. I watched him glance through the door to my body but quickly back to my eyes.

"If you have some I will." I smiled.

"Alright." He nodded and stepped out.

I giggled a little and finished up my shower. When I dried off some I stepped out. On the counter sat a pair of woman's athletic shorts, a big T-shirt, and a toothbrush. I smiled, then slipped on the clothes, wondering why he had a pair of womens shorts. I tried not to other think it and brushed my teeth quickly. When I opened the bathroom door, steam rolled out from the hot shower into the cold, dark bedroom. I could also smell coffee.

I followed the smell into the living room and kitchen. There was coffee in a mug on the counter by the coffee pot. I assumed it was mine and took a sip of the bitter liquid. It felt nice on my throat. I looked around for Kayce and noticed the screen door for the porch was open so I stepped outside. He sat in the rocking chair, just watching everything around. I couldn't help but smile as I watched him, wishing I could stand here and watch him all day. Per usual, he wore jeans that were lighter than when you buy them due to the wear. With it being a hot summer, he only wore a long shirt with a few buttons at the top that was tucked into his jeans. He was barefoot, pushing off the ground to rock the chair. And once again, no hat.

He sensed me standing there and looked over his shoulder to me. "Morning." He took a drink from his coffee.

"Hey." I nodded to him a little. "Not too bad out this morning."

"For now, suppose to get hot."

"Good swimming weather." I walked over and sat in the chair next to him.

"Swimming?" He asked, chuckling.

"Hell, if I was home in Texas, we'd go straight to the beach." I sipped more of my coffee.

He turned his head to me. "You work at the clinic today?"

I shook my head, "Just on call."

"Alright." He sat his mug on the little side table and stood up, "Take the truck if you need to go anywhere. Keys are on the counter. I'll be back later."

Surprisingly, he leaned down and kissed my forehead, then walked off the porch.

I sat there, wide eyed. It was such a casual thing he had said. Like he had told me this a thousand times before. I was cut off from my thoughts when

I heard my phone ring from inside. I jumped up and ran to find it. It was the clinic calling.

"It's Ada." I said, slightly out of breath. I downed the rest of my coffee and sat the mug in the sink. "Hello? It's Ada." I said again.

"Can you hear me?" Jeremy, our small animal vet tech, said through the phone.

"Yeah, Jer. What's up?" I scooped up the keys off the counter. Just like Kayce said.

"Well..." He started in slowly. I slipped into my shoes, jumping around, and trying to get out the door.

"Well what? What's going on?" I ran outside and jumped into the truck. I reached my foot out to the hit the brake but missed by a long shot. "Fuck." I mumbled, and moved the seat up. "Dammit, Jer. Either you're not talking or I cant fucking hear ya." I had lost all patience with this guy.

"I've got a horse here." He said quickly.

"A horse?" I repeated, confused and took off towards the clinic.

It wasn't long before I pulled up to the front door, beside an old red horse trailer in major need of repairing. I could hear the horse braying. I jumped out of the truck, not even shutting it off, and ran to whoever was near it. But my heart nearly stopped as I turned the corner.

I first looked at the horse. It was missing a large portion of the upper part of its mane and a little bit of the ear. Dark red blood stained the beautiful animals grey coat, along with drips on the floor. The poor thing. But it wasn't even the scariest thing I saw.

A familiar man stood, pointing a pistol as Jeremy was cleaning the blood as best as he could. The man turned to me.

"Jake." My voice caught in my throat. The man who hates Kayce. What a great time to meet again. I thought in my head. "Is this your horse?" He turned quickly to me, the pistol following.

He sniffled, and was shaking. His eyes were red and bloodshot. "Yeah... no. It's my brothers. You gotta fix him!" He started to yell. He was drunk or high or just panicking.

"Okay. Okay." I put my hands up, surrendering. I wanted to help the horse even if my life wasn't on the line. "What happened?" I slowly walked up to the horse. "Get outta here." I whispered to Jeremy as I grabbed the gauze from him, inspecting the horses wounds quickly.

"Stop asking questions." Jake mumbled and wiped his nose. Jeremy started to step out. "Where the fuck do you think you're going? What are you doing?" He whipped the gun around between us. Back and forth.

I quickly got in front of Jeremy,"Jake, he can't help any. He doesn't work with horses." I looked him in the eyes, praying he was sober enough to listen to me. He nodded a little. I shoved Jeremy away. "I'm gonna help him, but it's gonna take a while. Okay?" I whispered.

He nodded again, looking like he might throw up or pass out.

I started cleaning and taping and stitching. But soon I heard sirens. "Fuck." I mumbled.

"Cops?! You called the cops?" Jake shook the pistol at me.

"I've been here with you the whole time. When would I have called?" I threw my hands in the air, fed up with him.

"I'll kill you and your whole damn clinic and that little boyfriend of yours." He sniffled more. He was losing grip.

The sirens were getting louder.

"Listen to me," I said calmly, taking a step to him.

"Stop, there! Don't take another fucking step!" He yelled at me, spit flying from the corners of his mouth.

"Okay, okay," I stopped immediately,"Put the gun behind your back. I'll tell them everything's fine. And they'll leave."

He sneered,"Yeah, right. I'm not dumb enough to believe that."

"I'm serious, Jake." I begged him with my eyes. "I want to help you. I wanna help this horse. You said it was your brother, right?"

He nodded, looking over his shoulder and out the slits of the trailer. "It's all I've got left of him." His eyes became glossy. My heart ached for him. I knew they were bad people but in this moment, I just wanted to help.

"Let me take care of this. And if I've lied to you at all, you can kill me. I wouldn't blame you one bit. Okay?" I swallowed hard. This trailer was getting hot in the morning heat and the tension in here was making it worse.

He stared at me then slowly put the gun behind his back.

The sirens and lights came flying up beside us. This is my chance. I could run out and ask for help or tackle Jake or stab him with a scalpel. Anything. But when the cops turned the corner, with their guns pulled, I gave in.

"Whoa! Can I help you?" I asked, playing the part and taping up what was left of the horses ear.

"Are you okay, ma'am? Someone called and said this man had a gun pulled on you." The cop stepped closer to Jake. Jake furrowed his eyebrows and looked over at me.

"No!" I said, maybe a little too quickly. "Nonsense." I cleared my throat. "If y'all don't mind, this horse is in serious condition and I need to finish my work."

"Ma'am-" The deputy started in.

"Please, deputy. Let me get back to work." I spoke up. The officer nodded, in a confused way, not that I blamed him, and he stepped away.

Jake nodded at me as I finished up with the horse.

"He's all done. He may need the dressings changed, so gave me a call and I'll come out and change it." I tore off the last piece of tape then started out the trailer.

"He's gonna be okay?" Jake said quickly.

I nodded,"He's gonna be just fine as long as you let him heal." I wiped the sweat off my forehead with the back of my arm and stepped out the trailer.

"Alright." Out of the corner of my eye I saw him pat the horses neck and put his head to the animals. This horse meant so much to him. You could easily tell. "Hey!" He called after me. My heart thumped hard. Here we go. I turned around slowly, expecting to see a pistol pointed at me. "What you did with those cops," He paused and nodded with a dark look in his eyes,"That's gonna be good for you in the long run." He stepped off the trailer and slammed the doors shut. I jumped at the loud noise. He got into the truck and drove off, the rattling of the trailer tailing behind him.

"Ada!" Hannah's voice rang out, it sounded panicked.

I looked around for her. "Hey." I started to hug her quickly stopped, I was covered in blood and hair.

"What happened? We saw the cops." She shook her head and checked me up and down.

I shrugged as Dr Stone walked up behind her,"Just a miss understanding. Everything's taken care of." I assured her and squeezed her shoulder.

"You really shouldn't be working in shorts and...and crocs?" Dr Stone gestured to my shoes.

We all looked down, I was wearing the Nike shorts, big T-shirt, and mens crocs. Camo one's actually. "Yeah, I... I was in a hurry." I nodded, embarrassed as he walked past me and into the clinic.

Hannah gave me the "I know what you're wearing" eyes.

"Don't even start-" I put my finger up.

"Are those Kayces?!" She squealed.

I rolled my eyes and headed inside. "Yes, and so is the Yellowstone truck you're standing by, believe it or not."

8

-----------------------------------------------------------

A little while later, I decided I needed to take the truck back to Kayce. I was afraid to see him. Maybe he knew about Jake's horse and what happened. That man could see right through me if anything was wrong.

I took another shower once before I left, making my second one for the day. I let the cold water wash off everything. The blood, horse hair, and dirt. I tried scrubbing off the feeling of fear and terror that was instilled in me. I could have died today. Jake could've snapped and fired one, two, four, even six rounds into me. And everything would've been over then. It was hard to wrap my head around, almost dying. The worst part, I couldn't tell anybody. I wasn't able to vent and cry and worry to anyone else. If Jake found out I told anyone, he would come back to kill me. Especially, if I told Kayce. Kayce would have a hit out of that man.

When water wasn't helping anymore, I stepped out and changed into some Jean shorts and a tank top. It was too hot to wear anything else. I tied my hair up and popped on some mascara and fix my brows. That was it. Too damn hot outside for make up to be melting off my face.

The drive out to the Yellowstone was peaceful. It was a quiet road, not much traffic and on both side were fence filled with cattle. The Duttons cattle.

As I pulled into the driveway, I saw everyone gathered out side the bunkhouse along with Kayce. I parked beside them and got out.

"Hey." I walked up to Kayce, ignoring some of the looks I was getting from everyone else.

"Hey," He gave a small smile. "You ready?" He asked.

I furrowed my eyebrows,"For what?"

"To go swimming." He got onto his horse and held out a hand for me. He smirked.

I chuckled and shook my head, but grabbed his hand.

It had been awhile since I had been on a horse just for the ride. I really missed it. Riding with Kayce was a whole new experience. He really knew how to control his horse. It wasn't a rough, bumpy ride, which is what I was expecting. I kept my arms wrapped right around his torso and rested my head on his back. It felt nice to be so close to him. I felt safe- something I didn't realize I was needing but made sense after the day I had today. Within thirty minutes or so, he slowed the horse by a small river.

He jumped off then helped me off. He was smiling a little. He looked happy. I hadn't seen this smile on him in a while. But I was glad to see it.

I took in the view around us. The mountains were a gorgeous blue and had little snow on them now after the few hot days. The ground were rockier here, considering the River was nearby. It was also loud but peaceful.

"It's not a beach, but it's the best I can do." Kayce reached out and grabbed my hand.

I smiled wide. He had listened to me this morning. "It's perfect." I leaned closer to him and reached up to peck his lips.

He held my face with his dirty hands and kissed me deeply. His lips were salty but soft. I couldn't get enough of him.

But he pulled away and started walking me to the stream. The closer we got, the more excited I got. Like a little kid antsy to play in the water.

I let go of his hand and peeled off my shirt. He looked back over his shoulder and chuckled then did the same. I tried not to stare but can't help it as I pushed down my shorts. I could hear the same of his belt and buckle being undone and the sound was like music to my ears.

I walked carefully over the rocks and into the cold moving water. It felt amazing. Better than any beach I had been to. I looked over at Kayce, who was just standing at the bank, watching me.

"Come on!" I called after him, laughing in bliss.

"Alright, I'm coming." He slowly stepped in and made his way to me.

I was almost waist deep but could still see my feet. The water was so clear you could see a fish swimming around you every so often and the shiny rocks at the bottom.

"What do you think?" He slipped an arm around my waist, pulling me close to him.

I rested my cold, wet hands on his chest. It was glistening from sweat. I stared at it. Then my smile slowly faded. "What's this from?" I asked quietly, running my finger tips over a Y shaped scar, just over his heart. When he didn't answer I looked up at him. "What, were you just a stupid kid or something?"

He brushed my hair back,"Yeah, something like that."

I decided I shouldn't ask anymore questions. It was another question about Kayce that I was sure I would find out the answer in time. Getting to know Kayce was like reading a murder mystery. You learned his back story little by little, and just when you think you've figured things out- just when things are going good- something else comes up.

Things were getting too serious. I wanted him to let loose and just relax. To be happy with me and not so damn somber. I giggled and took a step back from him.

"What?" He chuckled.

"Oh nothin'." I grinned and turned around, walking a little down stream.

I reached behind my back and unclipped my bra. I slipped it off and tossed it somewhere up on the bank. I walked a little deeper in the water and held my breath, then dipped under. The cold water nearly took my breath away. I came back up quickly and pushed the water off my face and out of my hair. I nestled into the water, it came right above my chest. I swam towards Kayce.

"What in the hell are you doing?" He shook his head.

"Swimming. What does it look like?" I teased.

"Looks like I'm missing out." He walked deeper into the water with me.

I went deeper even further from him. Now I was treading water.

He got close to me, also treading water. I reached out to him, wrapping my arms around his neck, and my legs around his waist, pushing my bare chest to his. One of his arms snaked around my waist, while the other kept us above water. His warm body against mine felt like skin in the Texas sun. I rested my forehead on his, and brushed my lips across his.

"It's a shame." I whispered.

"What is?" He pecked my lips softly.

"That your hair is all wet."

"It's not." He furrowed his brow.

I pushed down on his shoulders, dunking him under the water. He came up laughing. "Okay." He wiped his eyes. "Alright. You got me." He reached out towards me, grinning.

"Wait-" I tried swimming backwards, knowing what he was doing.

"Hold your breath!" He grabbed me and I let out a scream as he pulled me under with him.

He was laughing as we came back up. "Not fair!" I laughed along with him.

"It's only fair." He held me right and helped me move the hair from my face.

A different sound filled my ears. The sound of thumping against the ground. Like a horse running.

I slowly stopped laughing. "Do you hear that?" I asked him. I readjusted my grip on him, pushing my chest to him more. Of course someone else would be out here as soon as I strip down. Please, Lord, don't let it be his dad.

He looked confused then listened. He nodded a little. "No one's ever out here." He grumbled.

I looked out around us and saw a few horses galloping our way. They were coming from the opposite direction we came in.

"Kayce." My breath hitched as I felt him swim back a little to solid ground. I couldn't touch the river floor but he could. And he held me close to him. "Who is it?" I asked. He had turned me so that my back was to them now.

"Jake." He sighed, frustrated. My heart raced. Great. He might tell Kayce about this morning. I hadn't even had the chance to mention it, yet. I felt guilty for not, but why should I? It was my job. The thumping got louder. "Don't say anything, okay?"

"Okay." I whispered, resting my head in the crook of his neck and briefly closing my eyes. I don't wanna die here. What would Hannah think of me? Her dads dying of cancer and I'm in a river, naked with Kayce Dutton. God, it would be the talk of the town for years.

"Shooo! What's going on here?" I heard Jakes familiar accent ring out and I wished I was invisible.

"What do you want, Jake?" Kayce spoke up.

"Right now?" I heard him chuckle along with maybe two or three others. "I wanna be where you're at."

I felt Kayce take a deep breath in and swallow hard. "You're trespassing." He said frankly.

"Am I? Then come out and get me." He taunted. I heard the horses shuffling some.

"Yeah, c'mon. Leave ya little girly friend and come get 'em. We'll take care of her." Another voice I didn't recognize said.

My stomach flipped. It was disgusting the way they spoke and acted. I felt Kayces grip tighten on me but he didn't say anything. There wasn't anything he could do in his position.

"Nah, we'll let them be. I spent enough time with her today, anyway. Thanks again, darling." The horses hooves pattered against the ground.

Dammit. There it is. I stiffened and felt guilt run through my body. My face got hot even with the cold water around me.

"Oh, by the way. There's some fencing down in one of your pastures. You might wanna make sure no cattle get out and onto my land. Cause if they do... I'll kill 'em." His low, raspy voice somehow got deeper and even scarier.

If at all possible, I squeezed Kayce tighter.

I heard the horses trampling and stumbling away. It wasn't even thirty seconds when Kayce readjusted me and looked down to me. "What's he talking about?" His eyes were dark and concerned. He squinted them some.

I wanted to cried. That was it. I just wanted to burst into tears. But that wasn't going to help anything. So I pushed through the lump in my throat. "The call I got this morning was his horse. Well... his brothers horse."

There. That's fine. That sounds legit. And it wasn't a lie.

"And?" He raised his eyebrows. He wasn't going to let up.

"And he pulled a gun on me and my coworker." I said quickly. He clenched his jaw. "And when someone called the cops he threatened to kill me, and everyone in... in the clinic, and..." I took in a deep breath,"And you. So I told the cops everything was fine." He drew in a breath. "But everything was fine! Well," I tilted my head back and forth,"It is now." I pressed my lips together. "Kinda."

"And you didn't think to tell me?" He asked harshly. He let out that breath he was holding.

"I just didn't have the chance yet." I tried to make excuses even though I never planned on saying anything until I had to.

"That's a bunch of bullshit and you know it." He shook his head. "We need to get going. Sounds like I've got cattle to move and fence to rebuild." He let go of me slowly and started making his way out.

My whole body felt heavy without him. I wanted to grab his arm and tell him to stay here with me. That everything was fine and we should enjoy our afternoon together. But not only did he have work to do, he didn't want to stay here with me. I could feel it. And it was the worst feeling of all. I immediately felt lonely again. It wasn't the only time someone walked away from me. I had grown up with it my entire life with my father. But this hurt more.

I pushed my hair out of my face and got out too. I got dressed as quickly as I could with wet skin.

Kayce didn't say a single word on the way back, or when we got back. I got off his horse and he took right back off. I watched as he rode away with someone of the others.

"Don't take it personal," A woman behind me spoke. It made me jump. I turned to look at her. Her blond hair was flying in the breeze. Her hair and make up and outfit didn't look at all like the rest of the people around here. She had a sense of class. She took a long drag off a cigarette then tossed it onto the ground, squishing it into the dirt with her black booties. "He shuts down like that to everyone." She look me in the eyes. She had the same mysterious look to them that Kayce does.

I nodded. "It runs in the family?" I asked.

She scoffed, "You catch on quick. I'm Beth." She stuck her hand out. I shook it.

"Ada."

"Ah," She leaned up against the Yellowstone truck I had drove back and forth earlier. "You're the vet tech that he had over last night."

A small blush flushed my cheeks. It was her this morning that I heard with Kayce. "Yeah. That's me."

"I hope the clothes fit okay. It's all I had with me." She winked.

I smiled,"Like a glove. Had me wondering why in the hell he had womens shorts though."

She chuckled a little. "With him," She shook her head,"There's no telling sometimes."

I stared off into the direction he rode. I could barely see them from where I was standing. Only specks of dark colors against the green and tan pastures.

"How do I get him out of this..." I searched for the words. "This quiet, distance thing? Everyone I know just drinks their way out of it."

She sighed,"Well, that's about the only way I know how to get out of it. Kayce's different. He won't drink his problems away. He'll just kill them." She shrugged.

I froze. I wish she wasn't right. I wish she was being dramatic. But after everything I've heard and seen, she hit the nail on the head.

9

-----------------------------------------------------------

Beth drove me into town and dropped me off at the clinic. I was ready to spend time with Hannah.

When I walked into the loft, it was dark and quiet. She wasn't here. I tossed my purse up onto the kitchen island. She was probably with her dad.

I sighed and flopped onto the couch. My body was physically exhausted and my mind was mentally exhausted. Today was suppose to be my day off, my easy day. And it turned into one of the most stress days of my life. I let my eyes slowly fall.

"Honey, I'm home!" Hannah's voice awakened me from my nap.

I yawned loudly. "I didn't even notice." I wrapped myself up in a blanket and rolled over on the couch.

"Get up, silly!" She tossed a pillow at me. My black hair covered my face as I sat up. I flipped it around, trying to see.

"Whaaaat?" I groaned. She sat across from me on the loveseat, wide eyed and excited.

"Let's go bar hopping." She grinned.

I chuckled,"You haven't wanted to go for weeks, Han. And you pick tonight?" I yawned again.

"Yes! Which is why you can't say no!" She jumped up. "I'll start getting ready." And off she went.

She was right, I couldn't say no.

Hannah was always more excited about getting dressed up and getting ready to get out than actually going out. We'll go out around 10. Drink two beers at one bar, drink another two at a different bar and then she'll be ready to go home. So we'll order pizza and pick it up on the way home. Then at home we'll take off all the make up and fancy clothes and eat pizza and complain and make fun of the nasty men that tried talking to us at the bars. It was one of my favorite things to do with her and the reason we got along so well.

I put on a pair of tight Levi shorts and a simple red tank top. I threw on lots of jewelry- bing earrings, bracelets, and a bunch of rings. I decided on my "going out" boots as Hannah liked to call them. They were pointed toed, dark brown leather Corrals. I took such good care of them, they still smelled like leather two years after buying them.

Hannah wore nearly the same thing but black Levi shorts and a white tank top. Her make up looked perfect and so did her hair. I had her help tease and spray and curl my hair and then we were good to go.

The first bar was busy and full of life. Hannah let some guy buy us a few shots on top of the two beers she had already drank. We danced and sang and drank for a while but decided it was time to move onto the next bar. And I saw familiar faces when I walked in.

"Ada! Hey." Jimmy waved from the pool table.

"Hey!" I walked over to him and the rest of the guys. I looked for Kayce. No where to be seen. My heart sunk a little. "This is Hannah." I introduced her.

"Howdy." Ryan tipped his hat to her.

"Hi." She smiled back with a flirty look in her eyes. I smiled watching them.

"How many games have ya lost Jimmy?" I teased.

"Listen," He put his hands up,"Colby's mom has had me distracted all night-"

"It's not funny, Jimmy." Colby huffed.

I chuckled and caught eyes with Rip. He smiled and nodded to me. Then he walked over to me. "You want a beer?" He asked, with a smirking grin.

"Yeah." I smiled back.

"C'mon girl." He walked over to the bar. "Miller lite. And whatever she's got." He spoke to the bartender.

"Millers fine." I nodded. "Thank you." I took the bottle from the bartender and put it to my lips.

I looked over and Ryan and Hannah. He was trying to show her to play pool. And she was letting him even though she was better at it than I was. She was doing the same to him as I did to Kayce.

"Seems like they've taken a liking to each other." Rip sat down on one of the bar stools.

"Yeah," I took a long drink,"I'll never get her home now." I shook my head and looked at him. "What about you? I'm sure you'll find someone to take home tonight."

He scoffed. "Nah. Every girl around here is after two things." I furrowed my brow at him. "Money and land. And when they hear Yellowstone, they think we've got it." He took a quick drink out of the dark brown glass bottle,"They don't realize wranglers don't get none of it."

"I see." I nodded, finishing off my beer and sitting it on the bar top.

Rip did the same. "So you picked right with Kayce."

"I haven't picked anybody." I reached in my back pocket. "Two more." I said to bartender. I started to toss money down. "I don't think he would pick me back anyway."

"Lemme get it." Rip threw out a twenty before I could get to it. "He'd be crazy not to." He stared at me from under that black cowboy hat.

I gave a small smile and took the beer from the counter. "You don't have to keep buying my beer." I teased.

"Shut up and drink it." He took a swig out of his. My jaw dropped and I playfully smacked his shoulder. He chuckled. "Darling, if I'm around you'll never have to buy your own beer again." He flashed that smile at me again.

He was either drunk, or real confident since Kayce wasn't here.

But Kayce wasn't here and he could've been. He walked off on me earlier and has ignored my texts.

"Okay, but can I at least try to buy you one back?" I leaned back onto the bar and blinked down at him with flirty eyes.

He put a tooth pick between his teeth,"How ya gonna do that?"

I looked over at the empty pool table. "If I win, I get to buy." I gestured to the table.

He chuckled and stood up. "Alright, then."

We spent the next couple hours playing pool. I would take small breaks to find Hannah. Every time I found her she was with Ryan but she would still go out to dance and sing with me.

George Strait came in through the stereo system and I looked over to Rip and Ryan who were standing at the bar watching us.

"Come here!" I hollered to them. Ryan laughed and made his way to Hannah but Rip just chuckled and shook his head. I loosely walked his way. "Come on. You can't tell me you don't know this song." I teased him.

"Oh I do," He grinned,"I just rather watch you sing it."

I playfully rolled my eyes,"That's no fun. Come on." I grabbed his hands and drug him out to Hannah and Ryan. He unwillingly complied but was soon singing Check Yes or No with the rest of us and dancing with me.

It wasn't long before they hollered last call.

"Well, guess we better find a ride back to the ranch." Rip smacked Ryan on the back.

"Didn't y'all drive here?" Hannah asked, getting one last beer for us from the bartender, as if either of us needed it.

Ryan slung his arm around her shoulders,"Well we rode with Colby and he's been gone a while. And I ain't got a damn clue where anyone else went."

"Y'all can just stay at the loft. I'll drive ya back tomorrow morning." I shrugged and took the beer from the bartender.

The ride back to the clinic was interesting. Rip and I talked while Hannah and Ryan made out in the back seat. They didn't even realize we made it back.

"Uh," I cleared my throat after putting the truck in park. They didn't stop. "Uh, y'all we're here." I glanced at Rip, who had his head down, trying to keep from laughing.

"We'll be up..." Hannah started, back was cut off by more kissing. "In a little bit." She giggled.

I shook my head and got out of the truck.

Rip followed me upstairs to the loft. "I'm so glad to be out of the that truck." I chuckled.

"You and me both." He closed the door behind him and started taking off his boots.

I threw the keys onto the counter. "Showers in there," I pointed to the bathroom,"Gatorade in the fridge, Tylenol in the cabinet." I flopped onto the couch, not knowing if I could make it to my bedroom.

I watched as he walked over to me and I felt him pick up my foot. I was confused at first but then he started to pull my boot off of it. Then the other one. He sat them on the floor. "Thanks." I smiled, drunkly and and tried moving to one side of the couch.

"You're welcome." He chuckled and patted my leg. I pulled them to me and laid on the other half of the couch. He sat down where my legs previously were. He positioned his hat over his eyes and folded his hands on his chest.

I grinned at how comfortable I was with him and stretched my legs out, resting them on his lap. He ran his hand up and down my calf, lightly. It felt nice and slowly put me to sleep.

# 10

- - - - - - - - - - - - - - - - - - - - - - - - - - - - - - - - - - - - - - - -

M y head. Tylenol. I need Tylenol.

I readjusted my eyes to see where I was. The loft. Okay. Good. On the couch. I looked down and saw Rip asleep at the other end. He snored loudly. I tried to keep from giggling and stood up. Oh. Dizzy. I wobbling made my way to our medicine cabinet and grabbed the Tylenol. Rip stirred on the couch. He picked up his phone. I grabbed a bottle of water and drank half of it.

"We probably need to get going." Rip groaned as he stood up.

"I'll get Hannah and Ryan." I yawned and started towards her room. "Han?" I flipped the light on. Nothing. No one. I chuckled. "What's the odds they're still out in the truck?" I hollered to Rip.

"For fucks sake." He shook his head and grabbed my truck keys.

Sure enough, they were knocked in the truck, but thankfully fully clothed. I let Rip drive so I had time to sober up before I had to drive back home. He pulled into the ranch and everything inside me wanted to die. Kayce stood outside the bunkhouse, saddling a horse.

"Fuck." I mumbled as Ryan, Rip, and I got out.

Do I say hi to Kayce or act like I don't even see him? I have nothing to be ashamed of. We're not even together. And Rip and I didn't do anything.

Kayce looked over at Ryan and then at Rip. Then to me and back to Rip. He clenched his jaw.

"Kayce-" I started to speak up but before I could say anything else, he stepped towards Rip and swung his fist around, making contact with his jaw. "Kayce!" I yelled, tears filling my eyes. I was overwhelmed by everything.

"Calm the fuck down, man!" Rip shoved him away but Kayce continued on. Rip returned a few punches.

"Kayce, stop!" I cried. It was getting out of hand. Ryan tried separating them. I grabbed Kayce's arm and he jerked his head to me. Once he looked me in the eyes he stopped resisting. His eyes widened as if he just woke up from something, just realizing what he was doing.

"Ada..." he reached out to wipe my tears.

"No." I stepped back, brushing them out of my face. "Why, why would you-"

"I just thought that..." he shook his head, looking between me and Rip. Rip wiped the blood from his lip with the back of his hand.

"Even if we did, it doesn't mean you can..." I swallowed hard, trying to get the tears to stop. What the hell was I crying for. I let out a deep, frustrated breath and stormed back towards my truck. I jumped in the drivers seat and waited for Hannah to get in too. Kayce jogged up to my window but I ignored him.

"Ada, let's talk about this." His voice was muffled from the glass between us.

I sniffled and started to drive off the minute Hannah got in. I flew down the driveway and onto the road. "You're right about him." I looked over at her. My voice cracked.

"I'm sorry, AJ." She reached over and squeezed my hand.

*****

Within the following days, Ryan had been coming over to see Hannah. It was good for her. To have someone standing with her through her dads illness.

Thankfully, Dr. Stone called in to have another large animal vet in the office. It made my life and his easier. The in-office vet, Dr. Teal, worked clinic hours with Dr. Stone. Helping him stay caught up on his current patients with routine vaccinations, pregnancies, etc. I handled mostly emergency situations but of course helped at the clinic as much as possible.

I ignored Kayce's texts and calls. There was no reason for me to keep believing I could make things work with him. We lived two very separate lives. I didn't handle the stress from his problems well, and I definitely didn't need anymore reasons to feel unsafe. I had plenty of those issues before Kayce was around.

Towards the end of the week, I got off of work, showered and started on dinner. Hannah wanted to have Ryan over for dinner but she's a terrible cook. I tried helping her but eventually it resorted to her drinking half a bottle of wine while I cooked.

I ate dinner with them quickly and decided to just go to bed. I was having troubles sleeping though. I either couldn't get comfortable or woke up every other hour. Tonight, I couldn't even fall asleep. It made things awkward because I could hear everything going on in Hannah's room. Absolutely everything.

I tried to block out the moans and groans by taking some NyQuil I had stashed by my bed due to the past few nights of no sleep, but it did no good. Eventually the noises stopped but I could still hear them talking.

"Yeah, he's been a real ass recently. It's just getting worse." Ryan's voice echoed into my room.

"She's not been the same either." Hannah answered.

Are they talking about me and Kayce? I sat up in bed and leaned my ear to the wall to try and hear more.

"Don't you think she's being kind of... ya know, dramatic?"

My blood boiled. What the fuck does he think he has any right to say if I'm being dramatic? I'm not dramatic.

"Ryan," Hannah started in. Please stand up for me. I prayed. "She's been through a lot. She's sensitive to these things. She saw a lot of violence at a young age, so she doesn't handle any of it well."

I let out a little breath. She understood. She really understands.

"Plus, I don't think her staying away from Kayce is a bad thing. You know how he is." She added.

I smiled a little. This sounds more like Hannah.

"I thought you were a doctor in veterinary medicine not in psychology." I heard Ryan teasing and Hannah giggling after.

Her happiness made me grin. She deserved it.

"I'm not a vet. Yet. Hopefully, Ada and I can go back in the fall."

I sighed and laid back in bed. I hope so, Han.

*****

"Ada?" Dr Stone knocked on the door to the exam room I was in.

"Yeah?" I turned to him. I hadn't seen him a while. He had start chemo and radiation. He was just skin and bones now. He looked grey.

"Can you go out to the Duttons? I don't think I can make it out there today." He gave a small, weak smile.

As much as I didn't want to, I nodded. "Of course. What do they need?" I asked.

Dr. Stone sat down in the rolling chair and in the corner. "Pink eye vaccinations. Maybe fly tags. I'm not for sure."

"No problem." I went over to the cabinets and started packing my supplies.

"Hannah said she's been seeing someone. Ryan, I think." He spoke up.

I pulled out all the vials and stacked them into a med bag. "Yeah, he's a good guy."

He got up, slowly and patted my shoulder. "Make sure he takes care of her for me. Okay?" His eyes were glossy.

I wanted to tell him not to worry about it. That everything will be fine and he can make sure for himself. That he will be the one Ryan asks before he proposes and that he will be the one walking Hannah down the aisle. That he'll be here when they have kids. But I couldn't lie to him.

"Yes, sir." I nodded.

Being at the ranch was bittersweet. It was nice to see everyone again. And they acted like they were glad to see me. And Kayce wasn't there. Thank god.

Rip was obviously in charge of the wranglers. He delegated them where to go and what to do. Within thirty minutes of me being there, he already had steers lined up in the gates, ready for me to shoot.

"That look okay for ya?" He rode up next to me. I pulled out my first syringe and vial. I started drawing up the liquid.

"It's perfect. Fast too." I pulled up the bar and let a steer run up to the head gate.

Jimmy was suppose to pull down on the bar and catch the steer in the head lock. But he was too slow, and the steer took off.

"Dammit, Jimmy." Rip cursed and wrangled the steer back into the pen.

Jimmy finally got the hang of it after a few more times and it wasn't long until we were finishing up. Rip insisted they didn't need the fly tags and I didn't push for it. My hands were already tired from the near 300 injections.

Just as I was packing up, and thinking that I had made it the entire day without seeing Kayce, a truck pulled up. John and Kayce both got out. They were walking up to the house and I thought maybe he didn't even realize I was here. But then he saw my truck. He stopped dead in his tracks and looked around. I made a v line for one of the barns and prayed he just shook it all off and left me alone.

I disposed of my syringes in the sharps bin they had in this barn. But I heard footsteps approaching.

"That's fine... A heads up before having a meeting with the governor would be nice next time though..." Kayce. On the phone as always. "Listen, Beth. I don't do well with those meetings. You're good at the legal shit..." I heard him getting closer. I took a deep breath and slung my bag over my shoulder, and headed for the door.

I turned the corner and was met face to face with him. "Ada... hey." His raspy, breathy voice sounded surprised.

"Sorry." I nodded my head and tried to walk around him.

"I'll call ya back." He shoved his phone in his pocket and followed me to my truck. "Ada, can we talk?"

"About?" I opened the door to the back seat and threw my bag in.

"I'm sorry." He looked down at me.

I tried to avoid his eyes, knowing I would fall back in if I looked into them. He wasn't in his usual attire. He was wearing a white button down and a gray suit jacket.

"Look, Kayce," I let out a deep breath. Just tell him. Tell him everything. "I can't live with how you handle things. I don't do well with fights and guns and- and-" I shook my head. "It's too much for me." I looked up at him.

Those eyes. They were sad this time. And tired as always.

"Okay..." he nodded. "What can I do?"

The question caught me off guard. "What?"

He pressed his lips together. "What can I do to change your mind?" I opened my mouth and tried to speak but nothing came out. I didn't know what to say. "As much as I don't want to be in this mess, I'm always gonna be. It's just..." he readjusted his cowboy hat, the same one he wore on our first date. "It's part of the family. But if I can... can help someway, I want too. I don't want you to walk away because you think I can't help." It was the most Kayce ever said to me at one time. He was a man of short sentences and few words. This was new for him.

I swallowed hard. "Walk away? You walked away from me. At the river. You gave up. You left." My voice cracked as I raised it. God, Ada don't cry. Toughen up. Just this once.

"I didn't know what to do." He spoke a little louder. "All I wanted to do, was put a bullet in his head. I didn't want you to see me like that."

"See you like what?" I asked softly.

He huffed, then shoved his hands in his pockets. "Mad."

He was saying what I wanted to hear. I wanted a man didn't want me to see him like that. He was exactly what I wanted. If he had to be this way, then please don't let me see it.

"You didn't care when it came to Rip."

He dropped his head, "Yeah, but Rip never did anything to you. I was just being stupid."

"Yeah, you were." I nodded and got up into the truck.

"Ada-"

"Kayce, it's done." Tears gathered in the corners of my eyes. It never even started really.

"No." He held my door open. "What is it? Are you afraid you won't feel safe with me?" He sucked in a breath just to let it out. He was getting hostile.

I wanted to cry now. "I'm afraid you won't be there enough. Kayce, I've never felt safe." I spoke slowly. It was hard admitting it to him. To anyone really. It was the first time I let myself say it. "I can't be alone. And that's all I've been since I've gotten to Montana." A tear slid down my face. I pushed it away with the back of my hand.

"C'mere." He helped me down out of the truck then pulled me to his chest. I buried my nose into his chest and breathed in deeply. He smelled like leather and cologne. It distracted me for a few moments. "Stay with me." He whispered. My heart raced. He's lost his mind. I'm losing my mind. "I'll be there for you at night and in the mornings. We need a vet anyway. You'll be around someone all day and if you need anything I'll not far away. Beth is usually at the house and there's always wranglers here. They'll keep you safe too." He rubbed my back slowly.

He was right. They need a vet full time. And I could always have someone around.

I would always have him. We could have coffee together in the mornings and dinner in the evenings. Take showers together and fall asleep together.

"You're crazy." I whispered and squeezed him tight.

"Yeah." He squeezed back. "Let me show you I can be different around you. I promise I can."

I looked up at him. "I don't want you to change who you are, Kayce." I reached up and rested my hand on his scruff covered face. "I just wanna see the good in you."

"You're being serious?" Hannah slowly stopped smiling. Her face became worried and almost frantic.

I sighed. "Yeah, I think so." I stared down at my feet on the wooden floor of the loft.

"Ada..." She shook her head,"I want to support you, and with any other guy I would-"

I stopped her. "Well why not him?" My voice cracked a little. I looked up at her sharply. I was annoyed by her. Everything she told me about Kayce had been true but she left out all his good quality. "What do you even really know about him other than all the rumors?" I pushed her further than I normally do.

She furrowed her eyebrows, obviously getting pissed at me. "Why don't you just take my word for it? What you don't trust me either now?" She leaned up against the kitchen island, folding her arms.

I rolled my eyes,"No, I just don't get why you never mentioned any of the good things about him." I flopped down on the couch, mentally exhausted from the past few hours.

"Because there's not many!" She threw her hands in the air and raised her voice. Then she just shook her head at me and grabbed a bottle of beer out of the fridge. It clicked against the shelves as she pulled it out and popped off the top. "You don't understand, Ada. He's not someone you wanna be-

"You let me go out with that dirty cop in Wyoming. And you knew he was selling drugs and didn't say anything. So why was he a not a problem but Kayce is?" Thinking back to those days made me shiver with disgust and embarrassment.

"Because he didn't murder people!" She yelled and threw the pop cap roughly into trash can.

"It's not cold hearted murder, Han. I'm sure if you really talked to him, most of them would be rumors anyway." I scrolled through my phone, trying to ignore her glares.

"One was my brother."

I snapped my head up to meet her eyes. "What?" I ruffled my brows. Brother. Kayce was right. Oh god Kayce was right. After the incident. He had said on our first date. "But..." I shook my head. "Your dad- He still works for them." I swallowed hard, trying to make sense of everything.

Brother. I've trusted my entire life with this girl and not once did she ever mention she had a brother.

She sighed. "I guess it wasn't really murder..." she took another swig out of the bottle and sat down in the chair next to me. "Not on purpose anyway." Her blonde hair fell in front of her face as she looked down to her lap. "I never told you because I didn't want you to judge me."

I immediately reached out and grabbed her hand. "Hannah... I would never judge you. Especially for something like this." I squeezed her hand tightly. As much as I wanted to wring her neck for never telling me, I didn't want her to think she would lose me.

She looked up at me slowly with tears in her eyes. "When I was 16," She let out a deep, ragged breath,"I dated a boy. And he slept with my best friend. Well," She paused. "I wanted to get back at him. So a bunch of my friends and I went out to this old barn that his dad owned and..." She sniffled. "We set it on fire." Set it on fire? For a high school boyfriend? "Anyway, we had fun with it. Unfortunately. I know this sounds crazy but I was young and stupid-" She started rambling.

"It's okay, Han." I reassured her and rubbed her shoulder. "We all do stupid things."

I watched as she swallowed hard and tears whelmed up in her eyes. "We kept setting other places on fire. Just abandoned buildings and barns and cars." She shook her head and sighed. "One night, we set one of John Duttons barns on fire. We thought no one was there but I guess Kayce and his brothers were there that night. We tried running away. And I didn't realize," She let out a shaky breath,"One of my friends, Mason, he had brought a gun. And he thought he could scare them away. To keep from chasing us," Her shaking hand pushed away the tears on her face that were now spilling out one by one. I was hanging on to every word. "He just shot a few rounds in the air but they shot back. They didn't hit anyone until we all made it to the main road. By some freak chance, my brother drove by and I begged him to let us get in his truck," More tears spilled out the more she wiped them away,"I told him they were shooting as us because we were trespassing so he got this gun out and was walking back to the woods. I just remember hearing Lee yelling to put it down but my brother wouldn't." She breathed in sharply but gasped a bit. "He thought we were the innocent ones. And the next I knew my brother was going to shoot Lee. Or at least act like it. But when the gun went off, my brother was the one who fell. Kayce shot him." She let out another long breath. "It all happened so fast,

I don't even remember what all really happened after that." She wiped her face with both hands. "I couldn't tell you. And I'm sorry." She sniffled. "I've just never been able to forgive myself..or Kayce."

"You can't blame yourself, Han." I whispered. I didn't know what to do or say. My best friend never even told me she had a brother. Not once. I didn't even know his name. "But holding it in like this, is not helping."

"I know." She swallowed hard then sighed. "I guess I just knew if you moved in with Kayce that he would say something eventually. I didn't want you to be mad at me."

I should be mad. You should be mad, I told myself. This woman has been my best friend for years and never even mentioned this other half of her life to me. Get mad. This is a lie, Ada. She lied to you. You told her everything. All the awful, terrible things that happened to you. And she never opened up. Be mad at her. You should be.

"I'm not mad." I gave a small smile.

It's not her fault. This was traumatic to her.

But I'm hurt. Hurt that she never told me. That all those times I opened up to her about my past and never once did she bring any of this up. I didn't know this girl at all.

"But you're still gonna move in with him?" She asked quietly.

I nodded. "Yeah. I am."

Because I feel like I know him better than I know you.

# 12

---

"T he Duttons asked me to stay at the ranch." I told Dr. Stone as I sorted through the X-rays of a pregnant horse.

"Good." He nodded once. "That view will be fine. Thank you." He took the one I had just pulled out of the stack.

"You're okay with it?" I asked him, furrowing my brows.

He took his glasses off and sat them on the exam table. "Ada," He smiled a small smile,"You could work at the Duttons and always have a job, never have to finish school, and make triple what any vet could. It's hard work, but you like hard work. You'll never have to pay for a single thing while you're there if you don't want to. If you can handle it, it's the best damn job in the world." The twinkle in his eyes told me so much.

"Were you their vet?" I questioned.

He nodded. "Until the kiddos came along."

"I'm worried about working for John." I confided in him.

He shook his head,"Nonsense. If you do what they want, he'll take care of you."

"Thank you. I still would like to be on call when you need me."

"Absolutely." He grinned and squeezed my shoulder. "You call me if you have any questions."

I nodded and smiled back.

*****

It was strange moving in with Kayce. I barely knew the man but I felt like I had known him for years. Everything I owned I could fit in the back seat of my truck, and it was mostly vet supplies. That Saturday morning I pulled through the gates and down the driveway to the ranch. The truck roared slightly as I went up the hill to the cabin. Kayce sat on the porch in a rocking chair, holding a mug of what I assumed was coffee. He smiled.

I jumped out of the truck and made my way to him. I smiled too. "Hey." I said with a breathy voice.

He nodded. "You need help unpacking?" He stood up.

I shrugged,"Not much there really." I walked back to the truck and he followed me. I opened the back seat door and grabbed my duffel bag of clothes and my boots.

"Is this it?" He asked, confused.

"Yeah," I drug out the box with my hats in it and handed it to him. "A lot of it is for the barn. Vet supplies."

"Alright." He huffed out a little chuckle and brought the box into the house. I followed him through the threshold and into the bedroom. I sat down the duffel on the floor by the bed. I sighed and looked at him, uncomfortably.

"I don't know about this." I swallowed hard. "This is weird." I sat down on the bed and stared at my hands that were gripping my knees with white knuckles.

He sat down beside me,"If it's too much, I can stay at the bunkhouse. Or there's rooms in the main house you can stay at if you don't wanna stay here." I looked at him. His face was sincere and worried. "Just don't leave yet." He whispered. "Please."

The cowboy hat he had on was the old brown one again. Stained and ragged. It was worn out for many, many rides.

"Can we go for a ride?" I asked. "Just for fun..."

He stood up. "Whatever you wanna do, doll."

I smiled again. I just need to get to know him more. And then it will all be okay.

We made our way down to the barn and saddled two horses. It had been a few months since I last rode so I was a little nervous. When I mounted the horse, it was like I had never missed a day.

We took off in a small gallop out towards the pastures. I thanked the lord above he chose this way instead of the large mountains on the other side of the ranch. I knew we would hit mountains in this side too but it would be a while and I could get use to my horse before then. It was the perfect day for a ride. The summer heat hadn't warmed up the earth yet. There was a breeze blowing and it made me ready for the fall season. It was cold air blowing, not sticky, hot air like Texas. My hair floated around me and didn't stick to my neck and face.

It was peaceful.

We rode for hours. Checking most of the fencing as he showed me the land. He knew lots about it and explained the history of the Native Americans well. Eventually I had to say something about it. "You must've read a lot as a kid." I teased.

"What do you mean?" He chuckled a little but it didn't last long.

"You sound like a history teacher." I chuckled some too, shaking my head.

He smile dropped. He just shrugged. "I probably need to head back and help the wranglers." He turned his horse.

"Wait-" I stopped him, catching his change in emotions. "I didn't mean that as a bag thing." I called oh.

"It's fine, Ada. I just need to get back." He snapped this reigns.

"I don't think it is. What's wrong?" I rode up beside him.

He sighed and looked down at his saddle.

"Monica's a history teacher."

# 13

- - - - - - - - - - - - - - - - - - - - - - - - - - - - - - - - - - - - - - - - - - - - - - - - - - -

It was the first time he really mentioned his ex wife to me. I didn't expect for it to hurt me the way it did. The look in his eyes worried me. He was still hurting from her. He still cared it seemed.

"I...I didn't know." I told him when we made it back to the ranch.

"I know you didn't." He nodded and got off his horse, walking her into the barn. I did the same. "She told me a lot about the land. She's native." He slammed the stall door and slide over the bar to lock it. Then he just stood there.

I stared at him. I didn't know what to say. How do you talk to someone about their ex wife?

Kayce's phone rang out and I silently thanked it for once. "Yeah?" He answered. I led my horse into the stalls as well. "Alright." He sighed, aggravated and started out of the barn. "Alright, I'll be there soon." He hurried towards the truck.

"Kayce?" I asked, confused and standing at the barn doorway. He was about to leave and say nothing at all.

"I'm sorry,"He shook his head."I'll be back soon!" He called out as he jumped into the truck and took off in a hurry.

I sighed and watched as he drove away. Something didn't feel right. It felt like something was wrong. But with his job, something was always wrong.

My mind started going again. Maybe I made the wrong choice staying here. Again, he was always in harms way and always had some problem to deal with. And it was never easy problems, it was always intense and dangerous. And he's still not over Monica clearly. I had barely been here for a few hours and I already felt unwanted and in the way.

I decided to push the thoughts away and started to unpack all my vets supplies into the barn. I reorganized it all and started flipping through all the horses charts. Most of them weren't caught up of their vaccines so I decided that's where I would start. I drew up all the vaccinations and then started in. One horse at a time. This spiraled into realizing the horses shoes were looking a little old.

Right around this time, Rip came into the barn.

"Ada." He nodded at me and headed over to grab a shovel.

"Hey." I smiled. "I've got a question I think you can answer." I wiped the sweat off my forehead with the back of my hand.

"Yes ma'am." He set the shovel down against a stall.

"When was the last time they've had shoes put on?" I nodded to the horse stalls.

He whistled a long pitch. "Probably right around a month ago. We keep a log of it somewhere." He shrugged his shoulders.

"Okay," I nodded and brushed the sweat off my upper lip,"Who's the farrier?" I asked.

"Whoever has the time." He shoved his hands in his pockets.

"You mind if I change them?"

He nodded,"Have at it, girl. You know how?" He raised his brows.

"I've done it a couple times and seen it a bunch." I walked over and grabbed the bag of tools for it.

"I don't mind to go through it with ya, if you want." He smiled that flashy smile.

I smiled back. "Yeah. I'd appreciate it."

"Alright. Come here." He threw his head over to the side, taking me to the first stall.

Rip finished out one shoe in around 15 minutes. It took me nearly 30. I didn't have the strength he had and I had to stop multiple times.

I put the horses leg down and stretched my arms for a second.

"Gets heavy after a while, huh?" He chuckled.

I nodded, giggling. "Yeah. My arms are getting sore."

"It gets easier." He winked. "I think you've got it down though. It's not too hard. Just takes some practice."

He patted me on the back and started to walk away. "Thank you." I told him.

"Anytime." He tipped his hat and returned a toothpick to between his teeth.

It took me nearly two hours just to finish the one horse. And Kayce still wasn't back yet. So I started another horse. When I finished that one, I started another. And soon it was dark out.

It had been nearly nine hours since Kayce left and I was starting to get worried. I pulled my phone out and stared at it, wondering if I should call him. Just in case.

Don't be needy, Ada. Don't be clingy.

I shoved my phone back in my pocket and decided I should probably just go back to the cabin. On my way to the cabin, I noticed the wranglers had set up campfire.

"Ada, come here!" Ryan called over to me. I grinned and made me way to them. "I heard you're staying around here." He teased and handed me a beer from the cooler.

I giggled. "I think so." I took the beer from him and sat down in the chair beside him.

It wasn't long before Kayce's truck rolled into the driveway. He drove slow and not very straight.

"Is he drunk?" Colby stood up, watching the truck go back and forth in the dirt road.

I looked closely but couldn't see anything inside the truck. It pulled up close to us and stop abruptly. The door opened but he didn't step out.

"Kayce?" I asked, standing up and starting towards the truck. Something was wrong. Something was off.

"Ada..." I heard him groan and then suddenly, he fell from the truck seat and onto the ground.

I started running towards him. "Kayce!" I rolled him onto his back as the rest of the wranglers surrounded me. He was holding his stomach. I moved his hand and immediately felt the warm liquid. "My god," my eyes burned and I touched around the wound. "What the hell happened?" I asked him

as his eyes floated to half open and closed. "Help me get him to the barn."
Ryan and Lloyd lifted him opened and ran him to the barn with me. I
shoved everything I had just organized on my desk onto the floor. It hit the
dirt floor with clangs and clatters. They set him onto the desk. "Someone
needs to get an ambulance out here." I spoke up to all of them staring at me
as I ripped his shirt open, exposing the gunshot wound to his abdomen.

"We- we can't get one. All we have is the helicopter." Colby stuttered.

"Then fucking call them!" I said a little panicked as I grabbed the gauze
from off the dirt ground. Colby turned and took off. I started packing
the wound. "You gonna tell me what happened or just lay there?" I asked
Kayce, teasing and trying to lighten the mood. I didn't want him to know
how bad this was.

His eyes glossed over. "I..." He was shook his head and his eyes started to
close.

"Come on. What happened, babe?" I reached up and held his face with one
hand while I continued to pack. His eyes opened and focused hard on me.
He was trying to stay awake but he had lost a lot a of blood. I was getting
worried. I turned to Lloyd,"Get Rip. And John. Now." My voice cracked.

Lloyd nodded with wide eyes and took off just as Colby did seconds before.

"Jake." Kayce sighed and his breathing became labored. That was all I
needed to hear. We could figured out the rest later.

I nodded. "Okay. Good. You did good."

The blood poured out more no matter how much I packed. I kept packing.
I had to do something for him.

"Ada..." It came out as a whisper. I looked up at him again. Those eyes looked sad and sleet. "I'm... I should've said... said bye. Earlier." He struggled to get the words out.

"Don't you worry about that." I tried to push out a smile. Yes. You should have. I wish you would have so bad. I cleared my throat and tried to push down the lump in my throat,"Don't say thing else. Save your strength." I wiped his forehead as the cold sweat dripped down his face. A bad sign of what was to come. His face went pale. God, he lost a lot of blood. Why didn't you call me? I wanted to ask. But why didn't I call him?

"I'm sorry..." He whispered again.

"Don't be." I smiled and held pressure onto the wound.

"I wanted more time with you..." His voice became weaker.

The words immediately caused tears to pour from my eyes. "Don't you say that. We're gonna get you on the helicopter and into a hospital. Then you'll get better and come home." My voice shook too.

"Home." He repeated and reached up to grabbed my hand. I squeezed his cold hand tight as John ran in.

"What in the hell did you do, son?"

# 14

- - - - - - - - - - - - - - - - - - - - - - - - - - - - - - - - - - - - - - - - - - - - - - - - - - - -

I sat on the porch in the old creaky rocking chair. It was cold this morning. Every morning was starting to be this way. Foggy, cold, and dewy. It showed me Montanas autumn was much sooner than Texas's. I pushed my barefoot off the ground to rock the chair as I held my coffee tight. It was lonely here without Kayce. I only spent one night and one morning with him in this cabin. And here I was alone in it now.

A black truck rolled in front of the cabin. Hannah stepped out and walked up to me. Ryan got out but stayed by the truck.

"Are you ready?" She asked, her blonde hair blowing in the cold wind.

I shook my head and drank the rest of my coffee that was only slightly warm now. "I don't know." I stood up slowly.

I stepped into the cold house and sat my mug in the sink. Other than that mug, the cabin was spotless now. All I wanted to do was stay busy. Whether it was horses, cattle, the wranglers or the cabin, I had to keep my mind away from what it kept drifting back to. It was easier that way.

I pulled on my socks and boots then met Hannah back outside. I jumped in the back seat of the truck. "John meeting us there?" I asked, sniffling from the autumn air.

"He said you and Beth could handle it." Ryan looked up in his mirror at me while turning around in the driveway. "She's already there."

"Okay." I sighed.

We finally made it and I pulled myself from the truck. I trudged through the parking lot and into the building. I felt my chest get heavy. I stopped for a second and turned to Hannah.

"It's okay. He's better, now." She must've saw the look on my face because she reached out and grabbed my hair.

I nodded, watching the nurses and doctors walk all around us. "He's okay." I shivered but turned back around. I made my way through the hospital and down the god forsaken hallways. "Kayce Dutton." I said to the woman at the desk.

"Yes." She smiled a too chipper smile. "He's being discharged today." She drug out the last words as she sifted through multiple files before settling one on and giving it to me. "You're his wife aren't you?" She asked. The question shocked me and I nearly choked.

"No. No. Just a friend." I shook my head, taking the papers.

"Oh okay." She smiled again. "I'll take you to him but we're asking to only have two guests back and his sister is already here. Did you want to come back or is there someone else...?" She looked at Ryan and Hannah too but they shook their heads. "Okie dokie! This way."

I already knew the room he was in. And when I stepped in, he smiled. A real smile. "Ada. Hey."

Tears whelmed in my eyes. He was sitting up now and had color in his face. He was talking and had no tubes coming from him. "Hey." It came out as a whispered and still managed to crack. I felt like I couldn't move but still managed to be shaking. I pushed my feet forward. "How-how are you?" I asked as I felt a few hot tears run down my face. I was always crying around this man.

Beth sat in the chair by his bed. She reached out and grabbed my hand. "Everything's okay. He's okay, now." She gave me a pursed lip smile. These small gestured meant so much to me. Especially coming from her. I let out a deep breath and pushed the shakiness out with it. I felt better.

"Yeah, I'm coming home today." Kayce nodded.

I swallowed hard and sat down on the side of his bed. "I know. We're your ride." I forced a smile, trying to tease him.

He grinned a little. "How's everything at the ranch?" He asked.

I nodded. "Everything's fine." I lied across my teeth, hoping he didn't see right through me. This wasn't the time to tell him. He needed to focus on getting better instead of cleaning up the mess Jake made.

"Did they..." He cleared his throat,"Did they find..."

He didn't even have to finish the sentence. "No." I sighed and patted his leg. "Not yet."

"That bastard. He's gonna rot in hell." Beth swore, shaking her head.

She was wrong. He was gonna rot somewhere worse than hell. In the deepest, worst place on the other side.

Kayce still had a difficult time walking. He didn't have much strength.It was obvious the truck ride was hard on him. The bumpy and rocky roads shook him around a lot.

Ryan hit a big pot hole, which he couldn't have avoided even if he tried, and Kayce winced.

"Are you okay?" I whispered.

He forced a smile small. "Oh yeah, I'm fine." He started to lift his arm to drape around my shoulders but quickly stopped when he realized it hurt too much. I gave him a smile and grabbed his hand.

When we pulled up to the ranch, I gritted my teeth. Now was when Kayce would find out things weren't really okay at the ranch. Lloyd sat at the entrance of the driveway, armed.

Ryan slowed the truck down and rolled down his window.

"Why's he out here?" Kayce mumbled and rolled down his window too.

Lloyd smiled. "Hey, kid. How are ya?"

"Fine." He cleared his throat,"You just walking around here with a gun for fun?"

Lloyds smile faded. He glanced at me. I bit onto my lip. I should've said something before. "Just making sure there's no unwanted visitors again." He nodded.

"Hm." Kayce nodded to and looked at me and Beth.

I dropped my head as they had their quiet conversation before we headed up the drive.

"Ryan," Kayce's voice was as strong as it was before the shooting. He had instantly gained back his strength somehow. Ryan looked up in the mirror at him. "What unwanted visitor was he talkin' about?"

Dammit.

Ryan stuttered,"Listen, I don't know if now is the time to tell you-"

"I run this fucking place. What the hell happened?" Kayce raised his voice.

Ryan stopped the truck. He turned around to him. "It happened really fast."

# 15

------------------------------------------------------------

Discretion: This chapter is a little gory and icky. Just a warning.

*****

I stood there in the pasture with everyone else as the helicopter flew away in the dark sky. It's red lights blinking at us until we couldn't see it any longer. What the hell do we do now? Go back to the bonfire and drink beer and wait for the news that he didn't make it?

Then it hit me. Jake.

"He said Jake did it." I looked up at Rip who was standing next to me. "I don't know what happened, or how-" I rambled on.

"It's okay. We'll figure it out." He squeezed my shoulder.

"We gotta... we gotta get him or something..." My voice cracked. "We gotta tell the police." I shivered from the cold air blowing through this little valley. I went to wipe my runny nose but noticed just before that I was still covered in Kayce's blood. I looked at my hands. It wasn't an unusual sight for me. I was use to the animal blood from surgeries or births or injuries. But never human blood. I stared at it and starting shaking.

"Let's get you cleaned up." Rip calmly walked me back to the truck. He opened the door for me. I stared in it. It was spotless. And I was most definitely wasn't.

"I'll ride in the bed. I don't wanna get it dirty." I shook my head and jump up on the tailgate. I assumed the guys would pile in the truck. But they didn't. They sat in the back with me.

It was a comforting feeling. We made it back to the ranch and into the barn. I stared at the massacre. The desks things and Kayces ripped shirt were on the ground everywhere and the entire top of the desk was covered in dirt and blood. Along with part of the floor and a small trail leading back to Kayce's truck. It was still running.

I sighed and stepped up inside the bloody truck.

"Ada, you don't have to-" Ryan started towards me.

"I'm already covered in it, anyway." I reached in and shut off the truck. I pulled the keys out and tucked in my pocket. The seat was stained red and it was all over the steering wheel and the door. A haunting hand print was smeared across the center console. There was even blood in the cup holder. My medical background told me it was likely congealing now since some time had passed.

The floor board had boot prints on the mat. Like he had walked through blood. His own? Or Jakes? Or someone else's? My mind started to run circles around itself about what possibly could have happened. Why the hell was he gone for so long today?

I had so many questions and so little answers. But I had plenty of blood.

There was so much blood. Everywhere.

I jumped down from the horrid truck and trudged to Rip. "He lost a lot of blood." My exhausted voice told him. "It's fucking everywhere." I shook my head.

"I know." He patted my back. "Let's go up to the cabin so you can wash off."

"I'm gonna finish cleaning up here first." I sniffled.

"No," He stepped in front of me. "Go clean up and I'll get you to the hospital."

I froze. Kayce's not dead yet. He was barely alive when the chopper flew off with him. But he was alive.

"Okay." I nodded and let Rip walk me up to the cabin. I rinsed my hands off with the water hose then went inside, hoping to trail as little blood as possible in the cabin. He stayed on the front porch while I jumped in the shower. The minute I was alone I regretted it.

I felt dizzy and scared. It felt like I wasn't in real life. I started to hate the feeling of the dried and sticky blood on my skin. I quickly tugged at my clothes but struggled to peel them off. I didn't want his blood on my skin anymore than it already was. I tossed the clothes straight into the trash. I stepped in the shower and twisted the hot water on. The water was cold first and it made me nearly jump out of my skin. The shower floor immediately turned red and shades of pink. The metallic smell reminded me of the first surgeries I did in school. You don't prepare yourself for certain things and the smell of blood was a big one for me. It nearly made me sick the first time. And here it was. About to make me sick again. Not because of the smell but the thought of it. It was his. He's not suppose to lose that much. It's not okay. It's not safe.

My stomach turned and I tried to hold it in. But I couldn't. I jumped from the shower, not realizing the pink watery blood trail I would leave as I got out, and hurled every bit of fluids in my stomach out into the stool bowl. I choked and gagged as my insides forced it selves out for a long while.

"Everything okay?" I heard Rip come into the cabin.

I didn't even care what I looked like. What kind of mess I was in. I wanted to curl up and go to sleep and not wake up. I wanted to wake up from this nightmare because there was no way in hell this is all real. I sobbed as I got sick again into the cold porcelain chair. I coughed and couldn't breathe for a moment.

"Ada?" Rip asked as he walked in the bedroom. I hadn't even bothered to close the bathroom door. "Goddammit." He muttered and ran in. He scooped up a towel off the counter and draped it over me. He was trying to protect my image I was assuming but it didn't matter because I was dripping wet with cold water and diluted blood while throwing my guts up into a toilet.

"He's gonna die!" I sobbed, spit gathering in the corner of my mouth.

"He's gonna be okay." Rips eyes were wide, tucking the towel around me. It was the most worried I had ever seen him. I can't blame him. I looked like something straight out of a horror movie.

"No! He's not! It was so much blood!" I held my head up and looked him in the eyes. "This isn't fair." My voice cracked.

"I know. I know." Rip pulled me to his chest and held me tight. "It's not."

I cried harder into him. "I can't lose him too. I didn't even get to be with him." I choked on the words as Rip smoothed my hair down.

"It's okay." He whispered. "I called Hannah. She's on her way."

I wanted to thank him. He knew who I needed right now. But he was enough for the time being. Someone else here to help me. I couldn't be alone. I didn't want to be alone with my own images in my head and thoughts circling through my brain over and over again. I was still shaking. I hadn't stopped shaking since the pasture.

It felt like seconds went by when I heard Hannah's voice. "Ada!" She yelled.

"Han!" I cried into Rips chest, still unable to move herself.

"Oh god." I heard her voice break into a weak voice. "Okay. Okay, girl. I'm here."

I felt Rip slowly move one arm away. "Please don't leave me. Don't leave me alone again!" My voice didn't even sound like my own. It sounded like a child crying for her parents.

His arms immediately returned. "I'm not. I'm still here." His raspy voice comforted me.

I felt Hannah squat beside me a few minutes later. "How about we get you cleaned up, sweetie?" She rubbed my back gently.

I shivered. I was cold. A hot shower would feel better. I was sticky from the partial washed off blood and unfortunately, maybe vomit but there was no telling.

"Okay." I whispered and tried hard to pick my head up from Rip. I did so. I started to stand and quickly held the towel to my body, starting to come back to my senses.

I was wobbly on my feet. Weak and exhausted.

I couldn't tell you the train of events after this. I remember Hannah helping me shower and redress. I remember Rip loading me into a truck with Hannah and Ryan. And I remember curling up in the front seat with wet hair, my eyes heavily drooping open and closed. I tried to keep myself awake.

I popped up at one point. "It's okay. You can sleep." Rip reassured me from the drivers seat, nodding his cowboy hat covered head at me. "I'll wake you up when we get there."

I nodded and drifted slowing back into a terrible sleep. Restless sleep.

It felt like minutes and hours later all at the same time. "Ada..." I felt a hand on my leg. "We're at the hospital." It was Rip.

My eyes shot open. "Okay." I unbuckled my seat belt and jumped from the truck with legs that mimicked jello.

I followed close behind Rip into the hospital and up the elevator. I didn't know how he knew where to go but I didn't care. Hannah and Ryan were closed behind.

We made it to a lobby.

John sat in the corner. He looked up and meet our eyes. I started towards him. I didn't know the man well. I had barely even spoke to him. But he meant a lot to me and to all of us. John stood up. I flung my arms around his neck. He stepped back some and didn't immediately hug back. But I held on tight.

He slowly put his arms around me and hugged tight. A real hug. Not a "I'm only hugging you back so you'll let go of me" hug. "Thank you. I needed that." He patted my back and I let go of him.

"Any news?" I asked.

He shook his head. "No. Not yet." He sat back down. I sat beside him and the other three in the chairs on either side.

It wasn't long before a doctor came out of the sliding doors and told John the news. They removed two bullets from Kayce's abdomen and one from the chest. One of the abdomen bullets had hit his spline and they were having problems stopping the bleeding. He was currently in the process of a blood transfusion and they induced a coma until the bleeding stopped. If it stopped.

John dropped his head. "Can we see him?" He asked.

The doctor paused. "He's in bad shape, John." He spoke softly but I could still hear him. "He's hooked up to machines and tubes-"

"Can we see him or not, David?" John asked abruptly and a little louder.

The doctor sighed. "Of course. Just, prepare yourself."

"There's no preparing yourself for when your son gets shot." John looked over his shoulder. "C'mon Ada,"He motioned to me. "I've already been through one dead son, lord don't make me do it again." He muttered as I trailed closely behind him.

We turned the corner into the room.  The doctor was right. He was attached to machines by tubes going down his throat and into his nose. Needles connected to tubes in his arms, pumping blood in and out.

John sat down in the chair beside the bed. "Oh, what have you done?" He shook his head and dropped it into his hands. There was that question again.

I couldn't help but think the same thing.

God, Kayce. What have you done?

# 16

------------------------------------------------------------

"You might as well go back and get some rest."

I heard Johns voice. I jumped awake. He was staring down at me in the waiting room.

"I'm okay. I'll stay-" I rubbed my hands nervously on my knees.

"No. You're not okay." John cleared his throat and sat next to me. "I've been where you're at. A lot." He nodded and looked at me beneath the brim of his hat. He took it off slowly.

I stared at him, confused.

"My wife." He nodded still. "And Lee, Kayce's brother. And a lot of other people." He let out a small huff. John was letting down a wall that I had barely even seen from Kayce. The more I talked to John the more I realized much how Kayce favored him. In the way they spoke and occasionally how they looked. "If there's anything useful I've learned it's two things. When someone offers for you to sleep, do it." He sighed.

"And the other?" I glanced down the hall at Rip walking towards us.

"The worst place to find out bad news is a hospital." He swallowed hard and stood back up. "Go back to the ranch, Ada."

My heart tightened and raced. I bit my tongue.

Rip shook Johns hand. They stopped to speak. And Rip dropped his head. Then John patted his back.

"You ready?" Rip asked me as he approached my shell. I looked up at him with watery eyes. He pursed his lips. "C'mon, kid." He cleared his throat.

I stood up with weak knees.

Hannah and Ryan followed us.

Everything I walked by was a blur. The hallways, the lobby, the elevator. The parking lot and even getting in the truck I felt like I was floating. Like it wasn't me and I was watching myself from somewhere else. Everything went numb. I tried talking myself into a positive outcome on the drive back but it wasn't helping.

Rips phone rang.

"Yeah?" I subconsciously heard him. "Slow the fuck down, Lloyd. What's going on?" I snapped out of my somber state and looked at Rip. Then back at Ryan. Ryan's eyes were wide and staring at Rip, too. "Goddammit. We'll be there soon. Call the sheriff." Rip hung up the phone. "Jakes at the ranch. His whole gang."

My heart pounded. "What for?" Hannah asked before I could.

"I don't fucking know." Rip mumbled as I felt the truck accelerate and push forward suddenly.

"I'll call the sheriffs office." Ryan pulled out his phone. I couldn't take my eyes off Rip.

He glanced at me and then back to the road. And to me again.

"Hasn't he taken enough?" I gritted through my teeth as Ryan was on the phone.

"Kayce's gonna be okay." Rip reached across and squeezed my shoulder. I couldn't speak. I was shaking again. "You're worrying me."

"You should be worried for Jake if he's there when we get there." I shook my head, all my sadness draining from me. Anger settling in now.

Rip leaned forward, opening the glovebox. It dropped open and he pulled out a black pistol. He sat it on the center console, staring at me.

I nodded, then stared out the window.

The truck raced down the black highway. It was so dark I didn't even realize the vehicle on the side of the road. I only noticed it when the headlights flipped on and pulled in behind us.

I leaned forward, looking hard into the mirror.

"Rip-" Ryan said.

"I see it." He mumbled.

I looked at Rip. His knuckles whitened around the steering wheel as he drove faster. He adjusted the rear view.

The vehicle caught up with us quickly.

"What do you have in here?" Ryan asked, unbuckling his seat belt.

I couldn't see Hannah's face but I knew it must've been shocked. It probably looked the same as mine.

"Rifle underneath you. There's a revolver in the pocket behind this seat and I've got a pistol on me."

My hands felt shaky. Something was gonna happen. I didn't know what. But something.

We drove a little further and it made think we were being paranoid. But as soon as the thought crossed my mind, it left. Rip looked into the mirror again, watching the vehicle.

I did the same. When I looked forward again, another vehicle was in front of us, a small car, stopped still. "Rip!" I yelled, grabbed the door for support.

There was no one in the car.

He slammed on the brakes and jerked the wheel right.

I heard Hannah holler from the back seat and Ryan shuffling around. I snatched the pistol off the console.

The truck bounced off the road and into the dirt shoulder. The front end of the truck caught a barb wire fence but Rip pushed through. He tried cutting back onto the road but the first vehicle caught up with us.

"Goddammit." He muttered again, looking a little panicked.

The vehicle, which I now saw was a white truck, turned sharply towards us, bumping the bed of our truck.

It slung the truck around in the dirt.

Hannah screamed.

I could hear Rip turning the wheel one way then back the other.

My head smacked the window. I winced.

Then I heard a loud crash. And I was raising off my seat. My world spinning around me.

# 17

- - - - - - - - - - - - - - - - - - - - - - - - - - - - - - - - - - - - - - - - - - - - - - - - - - -

My vision was blurry. And I was cold.

There was yelling.

I blinked a lot. And tried moving. I could move.

I felt dirt on my hands. I pushed myself up off the ground and looked around.

Then gunfire rang out. I flinched and hit the ground quickly.

Was it me?

I stayed there for a moment. Only my head hurt.

The window.

I looked up and toward the sound.

The Yellowstone truck laid upside down nearly a hundred feet from me. A white truck was on the other side of it.

I looked around me frantically. Hoping by some miracle the pistol landed close to me.

Black metal caught my eye. There was more yelling.

I picked up the pistol not even a foot from me, started towards the trucks, running crouched, as I was taught.

A younger man laid on the ground dead. But it wasn't Ryan or Rip. All I could assume was he's a friend of Jakes. Or was.

The closer I got the worse the scene got. Another man with a scruffy, uneven beard and baggy clothes held a gun to Rips head from behind him. The man looked terrified.

Ryan stood in front of Rip, his hands up.

Hannah was still in the truck, unconscious.

I flinched to run to her but I didn't.

The man saw me.

"Put it down!" He screamed at me about the gun.

But I kept walking closer. I had to help them. And he didn't scare me.

"He wants to leave." Ryan said towards me, his gun laying on the ground.

"Why the fuck did he run us off the road then?" I said more towards the man than to Ryan.

"He just wants Rip." Ryan slowly walked to the truck,"I'm gonna get Hannah."

I looked at Rip. He was calm, his hands out too. His right hand was scraped and dripping blood. The other hand also busted up but not nearly as bad. He was bleeding from temple and his lip was split open. He nodded to me. "It's okay." His voice was husky and strained.

I bit my tongue to the point a metallic taste flooded my mouth. It wasn't okay. Nothing was okay. "Put it down!" The man yelled again. I didn't know what to do. If Rip moved a little I could probably shoot the guy. But probably wasn't an option right now.

Rip spoke up. "I'll get in the truck, man. But she's not putting that gun down. You hear me?" Rip said the last part to me.

I felt weak. I nodded.

"She's putting it down. Or-Or I'll shoot you." The crazed man push the gun towards Rip.

I hesitated to drop it. I wanted to so bad. I didn't want to risk it even if he was bluffing.

"No! Don't put that fucking gun down." Rip pointed at me. I nodded again. "We can go. I'll shield you the entire time. She can step back. We'll go." Rip spoke to the man and started to move.

I could have good shot of the man. I was lined up perfectly. There was no probably.

But I hesitated again. Rip looked at me with wide eyes. He knew what I was thinking. And I knew what he was thinking.

No.

But I had to.

The man must've known too. I hesitated too hard. He took his gun from behind Rips head and started to aim it towards me.

I squeezed the trigger tightly, trusting myself.

And felt the jerk of pistol. And the sound of two guns.

I watched him fall and waited for my body to do the same. But I didn't.

I felt okay.

Rip hurried to me. He took the gun from my hands and handed it to Ryan quickly who had made his way to us as well. I stared at the body, red fluids draining from his chest. His arm twitched but I knew it was post mortem. It had to be. It was the perfect shot.

"I'm okay." I whispered. To myself specifically but also to Rip. "We're okay." I swallowed hard and focused on the man, making sure he didn't move more.

"It's over. You did good." He held the sides of my head, forcing me to look at him. I pulled my eyes from the dead man I just shot and looked at Rip.

"Okay." I whispered again. Still in shock. He let go of my face slowly, watching me. Probably expecting me to crumble at any given moment.

It was not even close to being over though.

"We gotta get to the ranch." I wiped my face and walked to the white truck. "How's Hannah?" I asked Ryan.

"She's awake and a little shaken up but I think she's okay." Ryan helped her up out of the truck.

She had a small cut above her eyebrow. She gave me a little smile. "I've been worse."

In the mist of everything, I smiled back at her. Im sure it was a crooked, hysterical smile. I chuckled actually. I think I was delusional. But I can't remember.

All I remember is loading up the two bodies in the white truck; the one that tried killing us, and taking off to the ranch. I barely remember making it to the ranch.

When we got there, everyone was busted up and beaten. The bunk house was trashed, the barn was destroyed. I couldn't even tell you how bad because it still wasn't cleaned from when we drug Kayce in there hours earlier. Some of the horses had been let loose but luckily, didn't leave any further than a few pastures away. We found them a couple days later. The main house was hardly touched, they hadn't made it that far. They were ran off before they could.

But they knew where Kayce stayed. They didn't care about the main house. They cared about his cabin.

I do remember the cabin. But I wish I didn't.

There was a blood trail on the old wooden stairs. And through the door way.

I started in the cabin.

"Ada-" Rip followed close behind me.

"Oh god." Tears flooded my face and ran down my neck.

Everything was thrown into the floor and broken. The radio he turned on for us that night, laid smashed on the rug. Glass was shattered from the windows being knocked on. The front door wasn't even attached to the frame anymore. The screen door laid half way across the room. Furniture was flipped and ruined. I didn't even make it to his bedroom.

Because Elliot Whittaker laid murdered in the living room floor; a box of roofing nails at his side.

18

------------------------------------------------

Kayce took the news well as you would expect.

When Ryan and Hannah dropped us off, he just stood in front of the place. I understood. I did the same thing right after it happened.

What the crime shows don't tell you, is that there's no one to cleaned up after a murder happens.

The sheriff and his deputies came and they did all their photographs and collecting evidence, but then they just left with the body of Elliot Whittaker and the roofing nail. It was group effort cleaning and fixing up the cabin. I stayed in the bunk house while we worked on it for the next week. Not that the bunk house didn't need work too, but it was better than being alone in a house with a blood stained floor.

I didn't know how to act around Kayce now. I wanted to wrap my arms around him and tell him it's not his fault. But I knew he wouldn't believe me.

I searched for words to say to him.

"Did they hurt you?" Kayce's grumbly voice asked.

It took me by surprise. "Uh, no. I-I wasn't here. We were on our way back from the hospital." I stuttered along.

"Right. That's when they hit you guys." He repeated.

I stepped in front of him, facing him. "We don't have to stay here, Kayce. I can go back to the loft-" I rambled.

He reached out quickly and hugged me tightly. I buried my nose into chest and wrapped my arms around his waist. I wanted to squeeze him tightly back but was afraid to hurt him from the injuries he sustained. "I don't want you to go anywhere. Ever." He pushed his lips to my forehead. I closed my eyes tight, trying to keep the tears in.

I wanted everything to be okay from here on out. That maybe the craziness would stop and we can go back to every day life. I can actually start a life with Kayce on this ranch, not just be here without him. We made it through the worst, and we're all alive. Kayce's alive.

I'm stupid to think this. Jake is still somewhere out there. We didn't have time to run a militia and a ranch. We were so behind as it was. The next morning I woke up without Kayce.

I checked my phone. 4:03. I rolled onto my back and sighed. I sat up with a dizzy head and made my way through the house. Kayce laid on the couch, snoring quietly. Last night he went to bed with me. He laid beside me and I felt safe. He had wrapped his arm around my shoulders and it was so comforting.

I leaned against the doorway of the bedroom and watched him on the couch. He was probably just uncomfortable in the bed from his injuries. I shook off the feeling and crawled back into bed for another hour.

When I woke up the next time, it was to get ready for the day. I didn't put in scrubs like I use to. I had traded in my scrubs for jeans and boots after the incident. They were short on wranglers so I stepped in. It had been years since I ran cattle, but I still knew how. I stepped out of the bedroom and made me way to the coffee pot. But I could already smell it in the air. Kayce.

I nearly kicked myself. I had forgotten he was back home. I was so use to being alone up here anymore. I poured myself a mug full and stepped onto the porch.

Kayce turned to me, like he forgot I was there to. He leaned against the opening of the porch, where the wooden stairs met the hard floor. "No scrubs?" He raised an eyebrow at me.

The edges of my mouth turned up,"No," I huffed a little chuckle,"It gets a little cold riding in scrubs."

He nodded. "Have you been wrangling?" He started to smile.

"Trying." I chuckled and sat down in the rocking chair. It creaked.

"I didn't realize you were a cowboy in Texas." His smile turned to a smirk.

I took a drink of the dark, bitter coffee. "I wasn't." I cleared my throat. My voice was raspy this morning. "But my dad was before he went off to the army." I looked down at the cup. It was the first time I mentioned my family to Kayce. He sat down in the chair beside me and reached over, resting his hand on my leg and giving me a hard stare. I went on. "He basically raised me until he left. I was 12 when he went back. He uh," I swallowed hard and had to clear my sore throat once again,"He had been in the army since he was 18 but he came back a little after my mom had me." I didn't tell him why. I wasn't ready for that part yet. "And then deployed to Iraq in 2006. He couldn't sit around and watch everything happen over there for some gods forsaken reason." I sighed loudly and stood up. I was over sharing and didn't want to talk about my father. I didn't even want to think about him.

"It's a strange feeling." Kayce stood up too. I stopped before walking back into the cabin. "Wanting... to go over there." He nodded.

"I'm sorry. I forgot..." My words trailed off. God, I felt awful. Kayce had been in Iraq too.

He shrugged,"No, it's fine. It's hard for the family. Hard to leave family..." He took the last drink of his coffee and slung the rest over the railing and into the yard. "It's hard to leave Iraq too." He walked past me and into the cabin. I followed behind slowly. He took my mug from me and sat them both in the sink.

"I didn't mean it like that." I said quietly. He turned to me in the half lit kitchen. The sun was just coming up and the pink, orange hue only slightly brightened the small house.

He held my face with his hands. They were warm on my cold cheeks. "I know you didn't." He kissed my forehead then pulled away to look at me. "Come on, I wanna see you as wrangler." He winked.

I giggled, rolling my eyes, and headed out the door.

Jimmy was feeding the horses when we got down to the barn.

"Morning, Ada." He smiled.

"Hey, Jimmy." I smiled back at him. He was starting to grow on me and I looked forward to seeing him in the mornings.

I moved smoothly through the barn. I knew where everything was at now and the equipment I preferred. I started to rewrap the banding on one of the mares. He was swelling more than usual. After wrapping him up, I lead him out of the stall then walked him around some. He walking fine but had lots of fluid in his legs.

"Is he ready to go?" Kayce asked over his shoulder as I brought him back into the barn.

"He's taking the day off." I pulled his saddle off and put him back in his stall.

Kayce stood up straight from the wire he was wrapping up. "What do you mean?"

I furrowed my brows. "It means he's not being rode today. He's full of fluid. He needs rest."

He opened his mouth but then just closed it, shaking his head. "Alright." He turned back around.

Maybe I was just grouchy this morning but it really pissed me off. As if it annoyed him that the horse needed a break. Or that I didn't know what I was doing.

"Hey, Jimmy- Can you make sure he gets enough movement today? He needs some stretching and a couple beers every few hours." I hollered out to Jimmy.

"Yes ma'am." He nodded.

"Ma'am?" Kayce mumbled as he walked by me.

I sighed. This was gonna be a long day.

Rip came in the barn shortly after. He patted my back rather hard, my body jolting forward a little as he did so,"Hey girl. How's he looking this morning?" He gestured to our swollen mare but kept his hand rested on my shoulder.

I brushed the dirt off my hands, and shook my head. "He's still holding fluid. I think he needs a couple more days. I'm gonna try some different exercises with him later tonight." I rested my hands on my hips.

He nodded. "Okay. Whatever you think is best." He rubbed my shoulder for a second then checked out the next couple stalls.

Kayce's phone rang.

"Yeah?" He answered it. "Okay... yeah... yeah, we'll check it out." And that was all. "Dad said there's some fence down in the back pastures. Have ya been out there recently?" He asked Rip. I sensed some hostility in his voice.

Rip spit on the ground and then placed a toothpick between his teeth. "Every other day."

"Suppose to be every day." Kayce tightened the straps on his saddle and started to pulled the horse out. Some of the other wranglers made their way in.

Rip followed tightly behind him. "It ain't you're fault you've been gone, but goddammit we're working our asses off."

"And still not getting shit done." Kayce mounted his horse. I felt my chest tightened. Things weren't looking good.

"Getting more done than when you were here. And for fucks sake, I'm down four wranglers. I'm working with what I've got." Rip threw his hands up.

"You've got a meth head and a vet, Rip. How much do you really fucking think you're getting done?" Kayce shook his head.

My eyes started to burn. I was trying. I didn't know what I was doing as a wrangler and I know that. I just wanted to help.

"Jimmys clean. He's been clean for a while now. He's busted his ass to get there. Don't call him a meth head." Rip gritted through his teeth. He was trying to be quiet. I knew he didn't want Jimmy to hear it. It would break his heart. "And Ada..." He shook his head. "I know you're mad at everything. And dammit, I get it. But that girl could've left- she should've left, Kayce. But she's here. She stuck around for you." Rip pointed up at him. "Don't get off that fucking horse until you get some sense back in your goddamn head or I'll put your ass back in that fucking hospital." Rip stormed off.

I stared over at Kayce. He looked at me, then looked away. He pulled at the reins of his horse and took off.

"Does it matter what kind of beer I give him?" Jimmy walked through the barn towards.

I pushed the lump out of my throat. "Just not bud light." I walked past Jimmy and saddled a horse for myself.

"Why?" He asked from behind me.

"Because it's nasty, Jimmy." I put my foot in the stirrup and slung my leg over the saddle.

It didn't matter what kind of mood Kayce was in. There was work to be done.

The next few days were long and restless. Up before the sun and home after it went down. Kayce kept his distance from me. I contemplated moving into the bunkhouse at one point but decided it would cause more problems than solve them.

I sat in the barn one night, stretching the mares legs and praying the fluid would release in the next couple of hours. I massaged and walked him around but there was nothing being let up.

"You're up late." Rip walked into the barn, securing a pistol behind his back. I glanced at it then at him.

"Yeah..." I sighed, rubbing my eyes and face. "I don't know what else to do with him."

Rip looked over his shoulder and around me. "Yeah, maybe you should go home and get some rest." He nodded at me harshly.

"I rather be down here. Kayce's been acting weird and he's gonna have a stroke if I don't get this horse ready by tomorrow." I shook my head and started to lead the horse outside for more laps around the round pin. Rip reached out and grabbed my arm. I looked at him confused.

He looked around again,"Go to the bunkhouse then."

I started to pull my arm away,"Rip, I really need to work-" The annoyance rang out in my voice.

Rip pulled me towards him, my arm hurting slightly in the process. "Go to the fucking bunkhouse. It's not an option." He said it so softly I could hardly hear him. He looked deep into me.

"What's going on-" My heart started to race.

"Just go, Ada." He gritted through his teeth and let go of arm. He ripped the reins out of my hand, and pulled the gun out from behind his back.

My eyes got wide. "No, don't. He's fine-" Tears started pouring from my eyes immediately as I begged him not to shoot the pour animal. I knew Kayce was mad about the horses, but not enough to get rid of them.

Rip grabbed the side of my face and shook his head. "Ada, calm down. It's not for the horse, hun. You need to go inside."

I was confused but relieved.

Then I heard movement. From the upstairs of the barn. Like someone was walking around. My eyes met Rips again. My heart rate that had just slowed down jumped up again like an atrial fibrillation patient. I nodded and let out a jagged breath.

I needed to get out of here. I swallowed hard and turned around from Rip. I closed my eyes and let out a small breath, taking small steps towards the exit.

I was scared to leave the barn. That Jake would be waiting for me to step out. As soon as I hit the open air I shivered. The breeze was cold. The nights were progressively getting cold and for some reason I had forgotten that it would be fall soon.

Then I felt it.

# 19

- - - - - - - - - - - - - - - - - - - - - - - - - - - - - - - - - - - - - - - - - -

I felt my body hit the ground. My head throbbing. I felt someone grab my arm. But that was it. My eyes closed and I thought I fell asleep.

I couldn't tell you when I woke up. Maybe an hour later, maybe minutes. My eyes burned and my head pounded. I was in a truck. And I couldn't move my arms, they were handcuffed together in front of me. I blinked a lot, trying to fix my blurry vision. I looked to my left to see Jake driving. I wasn't surprised. It was bound to happened eventually.

I sighed. "What do you want?" I asked, unamused, holding my forehead and with my handcuffed wrists.

"Don't take it personal." He lit a cigarette. "Want one?" He offered the pack to me.

"I don't smoke. It gives you cancer." I rolled my eyes at him.

He chuckled a throaty chuckle, "Yeah, something's gonna kill me before cancer."

"Probably Kayce at this rate." I mumbled, staring out the window, trying to figure out where we were but it was dark and everything looked the same.

"Probably so." He inhaled his cigarette and blew the smoke back out the window. "But at least I'll get my revenge first."

Revenge. I wanted to roll my eyes. How cliche. I would've laughed at him but I knew I was the subject of the revenge and didn't want to make our current standings any worse.

He drove a long way. And the further he drove the more nervous I got. There was no way they would find me soon. Shortly after my thoughts, he pulled up to a ranch I didn't recognize. He shut off the head lights and crept halfway done the driveway.

"This is where your lover hung James." Jake cleared his throat.

My heart started to race. There was house a far ways down the drive way and I wondered if I could make there.

"So what now, you're gonna hang me here to?" I asked, trying to sound as calm as possible while plotting my plan.

"Eventually." He sighed. Chills ran down my spine. "But I gotta wait for the boys to bring John and Kayce first." I swallowed hard and my stomach flipped. I was not letting Kayce and John watch me hang. I had to get out of here. "That house has a family with three little kids. And I'll kill every single one of them if you try to run." Jake started to toss another cigarette out the window. I wanted to think Jake wasn't capable and didn't have the balls to do it, but I wasn't testing it.

"You're gonna catch a forest on fire from that one day." I mumbled.

"You're right." He sat up with a evil grin on his face. He took the cigarette and pressed it to my arm. I wanted to scream. But I didn't want to give him that pleasure. I bit down on my tongue. I tasted metal. Blood. He chuckled,"You think you're tough, huh?" I didn't say anything. I was afraid if I opened my mouth I would burst into tears and I didn't want him to see me that way. "We'll see how tough you are." He then tossed the cigarette that burned my flesh out of the truck window.

It felt like hours passed by and Jake was getting antsy. He tried calling different people but was getting no answers.

Then a car pulled up behind us slowly.

"About fucking time." He grumbled while getting out of the truck. This was it. I tried hard to put a plan together in my head. There was no running for it. There was nowhere to even run. I couldn't fight him. I was handcuffed and much smaller than him. I couldn't even out smart him. He only wanted one thing. To cause pain to Kayce.

Jake jerked open my door and pulled me out. I didn't have much balance and stumbled to the ground. He jerked me up and shoved a gun to my back. It hurt up against my skin and I couldn't even imagine the pain if he fired it.

The headlights shut off and the driver side door open. A man stepped out, casually.

"It's a trap, Jake!" He yelled.

The man's body was knocked to the ground and Jake's grip tightened on me. The gun pressed harder against my spine.

I watched as John Dutton stepped out of the passenger seat and Rip stood up where the man's body went down. Where's Kayce? What happened to Kayce?

"Let her go, Jake." Rip hissed, holding a pistol up behind the car door.

"I'll kill her. I plan to. Whether I get to hang her like he hung my brother or not. She's dead!" Jake yelled. He sounded hysterical, he was losing it.

"Take me instead." John threw his gun far away from him. "You don't just hurt Kayce. You'll hurt my entire ranch. The whole state of Montana if you kill me." He held his hands up in the air.

"John. No." Tears bawled up in my eyes. It was all getting to be too much.

Jake shook me. "No, this is the plan!" He yelled again.

I heard rustling behind us. But I didn't dare say anything.

"Plans change, Jake." John started walking to us. "You kill me, and everyone will pay attention to you. You'll be the man that killed John Dutton. And they'll want to talk to you." He walked closer but slowly.

"Stop!" Jake yelled. I struggled to breath. I could die at any moment if this man unhinged.

"You can tell everyone about your brother and what Kayce did to him." John was feet from us now. "Just let Ada go." John reached out to me.

"Then they'll arrest him. And we'll get justice." Jake started to rambled and I felt the gun leave my back.

John grabbed me from Jake and a gun fired.

I screamed as John took me to the ground, shielding me from whatever was happening. I waited to feel pain somewhere. Or to become sleepy or dizzy. But I wasn't shot and I wasn't dying.

"Ada."

I rustled around and looked behind us. Jake laid slumped on the ground, bleeding down his neck. And Kayce was securing his gun behind his back, running to me.

"Kayce!" I cried out, trying to stand but didn't have much balance still because of the hand cuffs.

"You're okay, baby. It's okay. Let's get these off you." He held me face tightly. I knew my tears were streaming over his hands, they kept pouring. I had so many emotions. Scared but relieved Kayce was okay or at least alive.

"Here's the keys." Rip shoved them to Kayce.

Kayce grabbed the keys and with shaking hands unlocked them. I slung his arms around his neck and buried my face to his chest.

"It's over. It's over. I'm sorry." He held my body tightly to him.

# 20

----------------------------------------------------

My exhausted body curled up in Kayce lap the entire ride home. I didn't ask any questions because to be honest, I didn't care about anything else. I just wanna go home.

Kayce's arms wrapped around me tightly. One hand tightly held my side but only his arm caressed my legs, as if he was holding something else.

John must've waited until he thought I was asleep to say something. But there was no way I could sleep. I don't know if I would ever sleep again.

"Son, you can put the gun away." Johns raspy voice grumbled.

Kayce's chest moved up a little more as he took a ragged breath. "Rip said she was in the barn to get away from me." He spoke quietly, careful not to "wake me".

I bit my tongue. It took everything within me to stop him. He wasn't wrong. Kayce had been in a terrible mood recently. He was rough and short. We couldn't carry on a conversation without him telling me I had done something wrong or arguing about it. Not that we ever really argued. He would state his point and I would nod and let him think what he wanted. It was easier that way. I knew better than to argue with a pissed off man.

John disrupted my thoughts. "This isn't your fault-"

"Like hell it isn't." He cut him off. I felt his look down at me, making sure I was still "asleep". "Jake wouldn't have had anything to do with her if it wasn't for me. For what I did. I've put girl through hell." I could hear him swallow hard. I wanted to wrap my arms around his neck again. Kiss him and tell him I didn't care. I did care though but I didn't want him to know that. I just wanted him happy.

I settled taking a small breath in and buried myself deeper into him, wiggling my nose into the crease of his neck. I pushed my lips out and pressed them to his skin. He rubbed my side some and then held me tighter. It was comforting.

Kayce didn't put the gun down. He hardly ever did. It was rare for me to not see it and I slowly became use to having it around, not that I liked it. It was always tucked into the back of his jeans, or laying on the nightstand beside the bed. That was a whole different problem. He didn't sleep in the bed by me anymore. He slept on the couch if he was home. I hated it. I needed someone now more than ever. Hannah was too scared to be at the ranch. The guys at the bunkhouse were not comforting to say the least. They treated me like I was fragile and broken, which that had never done before. Beth also didn't know how to speak to me. John was the only one for a while.

The birds sang a little song as I drank my coffee, rocking in the chair in the front porch. Johns cabin had a better view than Kayce's. The porch was bigger too.

John's boots clicked onto the porch as he pulled the door shut behind him. "Been a long time since I've seen a woman sit and drink coffee on this porch." He smiled down at me. That's why I liked John. He smiled at me and no one else did anymore.

"I wouldn't wanna drink coffee anywhere else. I don't know how you get anything done with a view like this." I stared at the blue mountains. There were hundreds and thousands of living creatures within the crevices of those mountains. I wished I could see all of them from here.

He chuckled a little. "You sit here as long as you want. My dad built this porch for my mother. Always said, she liked to watch him come home." He sighed, drank from his mug, then cleared his throat. "It's not my business so don't tell me if you don't want to." He started in. He looked down at me, narrowed eyes. "Why don't you drink coffee from the porch at Kayce's cabin?"

I looked away from him and back to the creature filled mountains. Well sir, your sons been an asshole recently. That's probably not a suitable answer. I sipped my coffee. "It's hard to enjoy it when the person you want to be there with, isn't the same person anymore." That's better.

John nodded. "He was like that when he came home from overseas."

"What fixed it?" I asked nearly desperately. Just tell me how and I'll do it. John shook his head now. He turned around to go back inside. "Please. What helped?" I asked again.

He sighed. "Monica." And with that he pushed his way into the house.

My stomach flipped. It wasn't the answer I wanted or was expecting. I sat down my mug and started off the porch. I walked down the gravel drive and started towards the cabin I really didn't want to be near but it was the only thing that resembled home. I bit my tongue as I walked. Don't cry. You cry too much as it is. As I stormed past the bunkhouse, Rip came out of the barn.

"Morning." He nodded at me. I gave him a smile and kept on. "I need your help today." He spoke up.

I swallowed hard. Don't sound weak. Hold your head up. "Whatcha need?" I asked, trying to force a smile.

"I got some momma cows that need some help. You got time?" He removed the tooth pick from between his teeth.

I smiled wide. "Always."

I pulled my arm out from inside the cow. I pulled the glove off and tossed it into a five gallon bucket.

"So?" Rip and Lloyd looked at me with wide eyes.

I smiled and nodded,"She's good too."

"Damn!" Lloyd laughed. "All of them?"

I chuckled along with them. "All of 'em. I don't know how." I readjusted the baseball cap on my head and picked up my water bottle off the ground. It could've been rotten milk and I'd still drink it. I was so tired. I was tired all the time anymore.

"I think you're our good luck charm." Rip squeezed my shoulder.

I shook my head,"I don't think so." I scooped all my equipment and supplies and tossed it into my bag. I slung it over my shoulder and started to walk back towards the cabin as I heard a truck come driving up the gravel road.

It slowed down and park. I walked towards that way. Kayce rolled down the window. His face looked solemn as always. It was never that he was actually pissed or upset, that was just his permanent expression. I began to learn he got it from his father. But his eyes use to look a little lighter when he stared back at me. They looked purposeful and kind. There was dirt on the elbow he had propped up on door. And the closer I got, the more I could tell it had been a long day for him too.

"Hey." I smiled, trying to push aside any residual feelings. Don't ask about Monica. Don't think about Monica. It was just something John said. It's not Kayce's fault.

"What's going on?" He asked immediately.

My smiled faded. He didn't even say hey or how's your day been. Just straight to business. "Just making sure the mommas are good." I said softly.

He ruffled his eyebrows,"Yeah I see that. Why?"

He was being hateful and it hit me hard. I swallowed down the lump in my throat, feeling weak and upset. "Rip asked me to." I readjusted the bag on my shoulder and looked at the ground.

"Of course he did." He cleared his throat. "Hm."

I shook my head and turned to walk up to the cabin.

"Get in, I'll take ya up there." He called after me.

"I rather walk." I kept walking. Didn't even turn around to speak to him.

I heard the grumbling of the truck shut off and the door open then slam. I kept walking. Be tough. But soon I felt my bag get lighter and slowly being pulled from me. I looked up at the man with quiet eyes. Tired eyes really. Very tired. He hadn't been at the cabin much again this week. Not getting back until way past dark now. I assumed it was the livestock commissioner position causing these late nights because it was never to do with the ranch. It worried me. Every time he got back late I worried he would walk in bleeding from a gunshot wound. It happened once, it would happen again. We went straight from him almost dying to me almost dying back to normal life.

His dirty hands took my bag off my shoulder. I instantly felt inches taller and the aching in my arm stopped. "Thanks." I pushed out the words through the resistance in my throat.

He slung the bag over his shoulder then reached out and lightly rubbed my back. We made it up to the cabin as the sun was setting. The sky was orange and pink behind the blue mountains.

Kayce sat my bag on the front porch. I went inside and jumped in the shower. The first time I was in this shower I used mens shampoo and wore Beth's clothes went I got out. Now, I had my own soaps and loofah and skin care. And my own shorts and hoodie for when I got out.

I towel dried my hair and then tossed it in the washer to be done at a later time. I expected to see Kayce crashed on the couch, where he had been sleeping now but he wasn't inside. I glanced on the porch. There he was, sitting in a rocking chair but still as can be. You couldn't even tell if he was breathing. I sighed. He didn't look happy. He looked exhausted and angry.

I pushed open the creaky screen door. "Do you want to talk about anything?" I asked, leaning against the door frame.

He glanced over his shoulder at me quickly then back out to the sky in front of us. "Yeah. What do you want to talk about?" His tone was short and sharp.

It took me off guard. "How do I help?"

He sighed, then rubbed his jaw. He was either thinking hard about his answer, or trying hard to not loose his shit. I couldn't tell which one it was.

The silence grew louder and more awkward. I didn't want to ask again or ask another question. I just wanted an answer.

I stepped in front of him and sat down slowly in his lap. The rocking chair creaked as he leaned back some so allow more room. I pulled my legs up and draped them over the arm of the chair. He held my lower back with one arm and the other hand reached up to my face. He pushed my wet hair over my shoulder then held my cheek and jaw. "I don't know, baby. Don't feel like you have to fix this." I got a glimpse of the Kayce I know. This soft gentle side.

"Your dad said you were like this after-" he cut me off.

"I know." He pursed his lips straight. Then he was gone again. He licked his lips. "He told you Monica helped. Didn't he?"

I looked away from him, his hand falling from my jaw. Then nodded. "Yeah." I whispered.

Kayce sighed. "She didn't." I looked him in the eyes. Was he just telling me this? "I was a monster for what I did over there. That's what she would say. And she wasn't wrong-"

"She's wrong." I interrupted him. "You're not a monster. It was your job, Kayce." I ruffled my brows. I didn't understand how anyone couldn't see it this way.

"This-" he shook his head. "Killing people now, isn't my job anymore. And I'm still doing it." He clenched his jaw. His eyes were glossy. My heart shattered into pieces. I didn't want him to hurt. Not at all. "All I want to do is keep this place safe. You, dad, the wranglers, the cattle. That's my job. And I didn't do it." He spoke slow and quiet. He was being patient with me.

He was right. We weren't safe. We think we're safe now but what comes next.

There was no answer to give him back. There was nothing I could say to help or make things better.

I leaned down to him and pressed my lips to his. It wasn't a perfect kiss. My lips were chapped from the wind and he could've had a neater shave. It didn't matter, though. The kiss was warm and cozy. I felt my entire body melt into him. I wrapped my arms around his neck and kissed him harder. He tightened his grip around my waist and back. There was no space between us. This went on for some time.

"Bedroom?" He mumbled between kisses.

I moaned in response. "Please."

He stood up immediately, carrying me into the cabin and into the bedroom he rarely saw anymore, he was still residing on the couch every night.

He laid me down on the bed, and climbed over me, kissing me deep into the sheets.

"I feel safe." I whispered when our mouths parted for a moment to catch our breath.

He opened his eyes and focused in on me. "You do?" He asked.

"Yeah." I nodded a little.

"Do you feel loved?" He asked.

The question made my chest tighten and my stomach flip. "Loved?" I repeated.

"Loved." He said again, kissing my neck once.

I thought hard and fast. "Not all the time." I said softly.

He pulled away from my neck and sighed. "Okay." He nodded. "What about right now?"

"When you were kissing me." I started to grin.

He took his time with me and it was better than I could've ever imagined. I had been imagining it for quite some time now, waiting for him to make the move. But I'm glad we waited until we did.

I caught my breath and push my hair out of my face.

Then he did something I had never seen a man do. He chuckled, his naked body leaning on top of mine.

I hadn't seen him smile in ages, more less laugh.

I focused in on him, still trying to breathe. "Why are you laughing?" I started to laugh with him.

"You're a mess, darlin." He laid on his side next to me, still grinning. I rolled to face him. He looked happier now, more relaxed. I rested my head on his arm, and stared at him. We didn't get this time together much. I wanted to soak everything in as best as I could. His eyes slowly closed then opened again just as slow.

"You look tired." I whispered.

"Yeah." He pulled me close to him. "I don't wanna talk about that."

I nodded, burying my head in his chest. I closed my eyes and wished that moment would never end.

But that was the problem with Kayce. It always ended too soon.

# 21

---

I felt Kayce start to stir. His body was warm against my bare skin. The cabin was cold as usual. I inhaled deeply and stretched a little. Then I snuggled deeper into his warmth.

"I gotta get up." He whispered and lightly rubbed my back.

"You should just stay in bed with me today." I sighed and squeezed him.

He chuckled. It made me smile. I loved to hear him laugh. "I would give up everything to do that just once." He traced circles in my bare shoulders.

I propped my arm up on his chest and looked up at him. "When we're old you can." I said softly.

It was the first time I really thought about us in the future. We were constantly worried about life as it was in the moment, which isn't always a bad thing. But it is when you're worried about whether or not you'll be alive the next day.

"You think we'll make it 'til we're old?" He asked casually.

You think we won't? I wanted to say. But it sounded harsh in my head. I don't wanna argue. I want you to know I want us to make it.

"I'd give up everything to grow old with you." I played on the words he had just told me.

He didn't smile or agree. And that was okay. He didn't have to. At least he knew how I felt.

"I've gotta meet with the sheriff today. You want me to take you to the clinic and I'll pick you up when we're done?" He reached down and pushed my black hair over my shoulder.

"Yeah. I'd like that." I smiled. I liked the fact he was including me.

"Alright." He patted my back, gesturing for me to move so he could get up. I didn't move. "I gotta get up, baby." He chuckled, shaking his head. His hair fell in front of his face. He pushed it back and then put his hands behind his head. God he was hot in the morning.

"Ugh." I dramatically sighed and rolled over onto my stomach.

I heard him laughing as he got up. I smiled and closed my eyes, burying my face into a pillow.

Why couldn't every morning be like this?

His footsteps echoed through the room on the wooden floor. I drifted in and out of a light peaceful sleep. Like a Sunday morning sleep although it was Wednesday. The shower was on and steam rolled into the bedroom. I could smell the soap he always used. It was a comforting smell. When I came to the next time I heard him snapping the buttons on his shirt and then buckling his belt. A few moments later, I felt his body weight sinking the bed. He crawled up behind me and kissed my neck then down my shoulder and back. His facial hair tickled my skin lightly. He combed through my hair with his hand as the other arm held his weight off of my back.

I sighed happily. "You were in such a hurry earlier." I teased.

"I've always got time for you." He mumbled into my ear.

I grinned and rolled over. I draped my arms around his neck. He leaned down and kissed me gently. "If you don't stop now, you're really gonna be late." I peaked his lips quickly.

He smirked. "I know." His dark eyes looked happy for once. Thank god. I didn't know if I could ever make him feel this way again. "I'll come back to get ya in a few hours. Get some sleep, baby." He took my arm from his neck and put his lips to my hand, then laid it on my chest. I smiled a small, sleepy grin. Then off he went into the dark, cold morning.

I heard the front door close. I smiled at nothing specific.

This is that feeling again. That "grow old with me" feeling.

*****

The receptionist at the clinic greeted me as I pushed past the door leading to our exam rooms. Hannah leaned against the wall, staring at an X-ray all lit up.

"That's a hell of a break." I mumbled, standing beside her.

She jumped and turned to me. "Hey!" She grinned and hugged me.

"Hey, Han." I squeezed her. God, I missed her.

"I didn't know you were coming in today." She let me go and her blonde curls flowed back behind her shoulders, over the blue scrubs she had on. I missed wearing my scrubs. I still could if I wanted to but it wasn't practical at the ranch. I never knew what I would get into.

"Figured I might as well swing by. Kayce had to come into town anyway so he just threw me out here. What are we looking at?" I put my attention back to the X-ray.

I helped Hannah with her work load. It was heavier today, since Dr. Stone was out. She said he rarely works. He was so weak and so tired from all the treatments. But she insisted he or herself didn't need the help.

I was stitching up a laceration on a mule in the one outside when Kayce showed up.

"Need any help?" He asked, leaning on the gate.

"Yeah, how good are you at sutures?" I squinted my eyes through the sun peering down at us.

"Not." He huffed.

I smiled a little and took my time finishing up the stitches.

"How long do those stay in for?" Kayce spoke up, still leaning at the gate.

I was surprised he took interest or even cared. Maybe he didn't and just wanted to make conversation. "These are dissolving stitches so a week or so and then they should be fine."

"You don't take them out?" He furrowed his brow.

I shook my head. "Nope. They absorb and disintegrate." I started to lead the mule onto of the pin.

"The ones at the ranch you have to remove, though?" He walked beside me. I nodded and opened the trailer door. I hoped in and led the mule back. "Well, can we use these on the cattle?"

"Yeah, we could use them on humans if we wanted." I grunted while I closed the door. I pushed on the latch but it was stuck. I leaned all my weight into it but it still didn't budge. I stared at it for a second. We could use them on humans. I hated that I was thinking that way. Thinking that I may having to stitch someone up.

Kayce reached around me and pushed the latch closed, without much effort. "I'll see if we can get you those instead. Make your life a little easier."

"Thanks." I said with a breathy voice, trying to push out my thoughts.

I went inside and wrapped up with what I was doing. I hugged Hannah tight. "Call me if you need anything."

"I always do." She groaned.

Someone called her name. "Go." I let go of her and have her a smile.

"Dinner soon!" She called after me.

I gave her a thumbs up and headed out to Kayce's truck. He leaned against my door. "You ready?" He asked. I nodded. He opened my door for me and I climbed in.

He strode around the front of the truck and then got in. "I gotta stop somewhere on the way back." He pulled down on the gear shift and put the truck in drive.

"Okay." I pulled my knees up to my chest and leaned forward to turn up the radio.

"How's Hannah?" He asked over the music.

I shrugged. "She says she's fine but I wouldn't be. She's gotta be exhausted." I shook my head. I felt bad for her. Her bad had always been there for her and now it didn't look like he would be around much longer.

Kayce nodded, "Any updates on him?" Referring to Dr Stone.

I shook my head no, "Just a matter of time."

Kayce made his stop at a ranch and spent some time there. Then we went back to the Yellowstone. Something was obviously wrong when we pulled in the drive. There were a few saddled horses tied up but no one on them. They were all gathered around a pen.

"Kayce, stop." I said softly.

"What's wrong?" He slowed down.

Then I saw Rip and Walker in the pen. Both bloody and staggering.

I pulled up on the trucks door handle but it was locked. "Stop the fucking truck." My shaky hands danced around the unlock button until it finally made the clicking sound. The truck stopped immediately and Kayce flung his door open once he realized what was going on. I bailed out of the truck after him.

Fights were normal. And it's fine. Sometimes it's good to have a fight every once in a while. But Rip fighting, was never a good thing.

"Hey!" Kayce's deep voice yelled as he pushed through the crowd of wranglers and jumped up onto the gate.

"What happened?" I asked, slightly out of the breath to Ryan and Colby.

Kayce's feet hit the dirt on the other side as Walker was swinging to Rip again. Rip ducked and returned the punch, blood spraying around them and grunts from either party.

"That's enough!" Kayce grabbed Rips coat by the shoulders and guided him towards the edge of the pen, leaving Walker on the ground. "What the fuck is going on?!" Kayce roughly let go of him. Normally, Rip wouldn't have moved much but this must be towards the end of the fight because he unsteadily caught the pipe fence for balance.

"Ask him what he fucking said." Rip spat blood out onto the ground.

I saw a clot of blood gush from his forehead.

"Oh my god." I mumbled and ran towards the truck. I grabbed my vet bag as more words were exchanged. I pushed my way over to Rip. He saw me and shook his head.

"Get out of here." He mumbled.

"Your head looks terrible." I pulled out some gauze and poured rubbing alcohol over it.

Rip leaned forward onto the fence. "It doesn't matter. Get the fuck out of here. Kayce's about to get pissed."

My heart started pounding in my ears. "What did Walker say?" It came out as a whisper.

Rip shook his head, then spit blood out onto the ground. "Ryan-" Rip gestured him to come over. Ryan hurried to us. "Take her home. Now." He growled.

Ryan nodded. "C'mon." He put his hand on my back and tried to gestured me away.

"No." I stepped away. "What did he say?" I said a little louder to Rip. It got quiet for a moment. Everyone was staring at me. "What did he say that was that bad?" My voice strained. I didn't think there was anything he could've said to piss Rip off this much.

"It doesn't matter. You need to go home." Rip started in again. But his words were tired and heavy.

Walker stumbled up to his feet. "Hell she ain't even got a home. She ain't welcome home. Your mommas was a whore at the Sixes and your daddy's in the ground cause of you."

Before he got the words out Kayce's fist connected with his jaw and sent him back to the ground. Kayce looked down at him then over at me. "I'll be fucking back." He grumbled and then walked over to me. As he came closer, he scolded the guys. "What the fuck is everyone standing around for? There's a camp that needs to be set up, cattle the needs to be moved, and I'm sure that fucking fence ain't been touched yet! Get to work, dammit." He shook his head then grabbed Rips shoulder. "Don't let him get up. I'll be back in a few minutes."

I swallowed hard when he looked at me. "Let's get you home, darlin'."

# 22

- - - - - - - - - - - - - - - - - - - - - - - - - - - - - - - - - - - - - - - - -

"What he said wasn't wrong." I took a swig from my beer. The old rocking chair creaked against the floor boards of the porch. It was too cold to be outside in the evenings anymore. I wanted to talk Kayce into getting us a propane stand up heater so I could stay out here without shivering.

The dusk sun was setting behind Kayce as he appeared in my view on the steps. I couldn't look at him though. He was about to know all my secrets.

"Ada-" He shook his head as he walked up the stairs.

"I know you think you're a bad man, Kayce. But you're not." I sighed. "My dad was a bad man. He was a traumatized old army vet. Who hated my mother and had every right to but shouldn't have been left alone to raise a daughter."

Kayce kneeled down in front of me and rested his hands on my knees. "We don't have to do this now. We can talk when you're ready."

I responded immediately. "I'll never be ready."

"I can wait until then." He face was somber again. Typical Kayce. The kind of face that doesn't budge when he speaks. Only those big browns eyes and his lips move when he says something serious.

I bit my tongue between my teeth. "Thats really not fair to you. I've heard all your dark secrets. I shouldn't keep mine from you." I reached out and held the side of his face with my cold hand.

He sighed and removed his cowboy hat, tossing it onto the chair beside us. "You haven't even heard the start of 'em baby. We'll talk when you want to." He patted my leg and then stood up. "What are we thinking for dinner?" He kissed my forehead quickly and then started instead.

"Is he alive?" I asked, my voice cracking. I looked over my shoulder at him. "Did you kill Walker?"

"No." He clenched his jaw after he said it. It made me worried. "I'm trying to work on that."

I couldn't help but break into a little smile. It was inappropriate timing but it made my chuckle. Maybe it was the stress getting to me and making me delusional.

"Oh, god Kayce." I shook my head, still chuckling and stood up. "Most husbands try to work on their jealousy or not taking the trash out but no. Not mine." I grinned as I met him at the door way.

He was grinning now. "You realize what you said?"

I furrowed my brow and tried to think. "What, did you not take out the trash?" I glanced around him at the trash bin.

Kayce reached out and grabbed my waist, pulling me close to him. He smiled a glowing grin. "You said husband."

"Well..." I bit my tongue. "What am I suppose to call you?" I glanced at his lips. That was dry and cracked from the cold winter winds. So were mine.

He smoothed my hair down and held my cheek. "Whatever you want." His raspy breath humbled me.

I felt my chest tightened. The thing I want to call him. Mine was the first I could think of. But that was cliche. He isn't a cliche man. He's different and special.

I would call him strong. And faithful. And brave. And loving and caring and kind. I would call him the most perfect unperfect man. He had been through some of the worst things I couldn't even imagine and still manages to be so tender at heart. How could such a dangerous and harsh man be so gentle to me?

"How about just Kayce?" I whispered.

"Yeah. That's fine." The corners of his mouth turned upwards. He leaned down and pecked my lips. "Come inside. It's cold and I'm hungry."

"Whatcha want?" I passed by him into the house and opened the fridge. There wasn't much to choose from.

He reached around me and grabbed a beer. The glass bottle clicked and tinked against the shelf as he pulled it out. "Whatever's easy for you, darlin'. I'm gonna take a shower." He kissed my cheek.

"Good. You stink." I teased as he started to walk away.

"Yeah and you smell any better?" He popped open the beer and took a drink from it.

I rolled my eyes playfully. "I do need one."

His eyes narrowed. "C'mon then." He tossed his head in the direction of the bedroom.

My heart raced. I bit my lip. "I need to start dinner." I shook my head, grinning and blushing.

He sat the beer on the island and I soon felt his body press against my back. He reached around and grabbed my breast. "I want dessert first." He whispered in my ear and squeezed tight.

"Kayce!" I squealed, laughing, and slipping from his grip.

He chuckled and snaked his arms around my waist, not letting me escape-not that I would want to. "What's wrong? You don't wanna?" He started kissing on my neck. I giggled and turned around in his arms, now facing him. A smirk was plastered to his face. He licked his lips then pressed them together.

"And see you all wet and naked in a hot shower? Absolutely not." I smiled and I reached up, pushing my lips to his. He kissed me back deeply.

He pulled away, grinning and grabbed my hand, leading me to the shower.

He reached in the bathroom and turned the hot water on. He pulled off his shirt and I saw the multiple scars. I knew they were there and I had seen them a lot. He told me how he got most of them and it made me feel guilty. As he unbuckled his belt and unzipped his jeans, he noticed my change in mood.

"What's a matter?" He ruffled his brow and looked at down at his abdomen. "Do the scars still bother you?" He came closer and put his hands my shoulders. He rubbed down my arms and back up.

I swallowed hard and shook my head. "I mean, yeah a little. I just..." I sighed. "I have some too."

"Okay." He nodded. "Let me see." I pulled off my thermal shirt and turned around. I closed my eyes and waited for him to say something. But he didn't.

I felt his lips touch my skin where I knew the scars still where. He knelt down and kissed across my lower back, holding my hips and then rubbing my thighs. It was relaxing. He stood back up and kissed my shoulders as he unclipped my bra. I slipped it off and leaned back into him. He kissed into my neck.

"I don't care if you have old scars. We've all got them." He ran his rough hands down my stomach and to the top of my jeans. He undid with the button. "But you'll never have any new ones as long as I'm here." I closed my eyes tight, trying to push away any tears. Just tears of relief and old sadness. "You hear me?" He grumbled in my ear and rested his head against mine.

"Yeah." I whispered, the weakness in my voice cracking through.

"Just relax. Let me take care of you, baby." His deep growl melted me.

I took a deep breath and as I let it out I felt a huge weight fall off me. As if he had somehow taken it all away with just his words and touch.

**23**

----

Montana winters were long. Longer than I was use to. It made it hard to get things done when all I wanted to do was stay warm. The cold air was brutal, even in the barns. And it didn't matter how many layers of thermals or gloves or socks you put on, something still got cold. And the snow. It made everything wet and muddy and slippery. It was a mess all the time.

I slung around the heavy jugs of dewormer. Maybe it wasn't the ideal weather for this but these cattle couldn't wait any longer. It wasn't rainy or snowing today, just cold. The coldest it had felt in a while.

"How many?"

The voice echoed into the barn. Kayce. I grinned and looked out from behind the stall.

He leaned against the doorframe, looking out to the round pens. His phone pressed up to his ear and his hand shoved in my pocket. I stared at the familiar view. It wasn't even a year ago, I saw him there in the same position. He was cussing about not having enough horses. Then the next time I showed up, I got a real view of how he was to others. Harsh and impatient, until he realized it was me. Then he was caring and kind and sweet. He is two completely different people at times. I'm just thankful I get to see the good one.

"Alright. I'll be there."

He shoved the phone into his pocket and then hung his head and sighed.

I walked up to him quietly and spoke right before I rested my head on his back. "Everything okay?" I reached around and ran my hand across his chest.

"Everything's fine, baby." He grabbed my hand and squeezed. "What are you up to today?"

"Gonna start dewormer." I sighed.

He turned around and pulled me close to him. "Have one of the wranglers help ya. It's too cold for you to be out here too long." He pushed my hair over my shoulder.

I grinned a little smile at his over protectiveness. "I'll be fine, Kayce."

"No, I'm serious." He shook his head. "It's gonna get under 0 today. We're suppose to get a bad snow tonight."

I ruffled my brows. "Under zero?" I repeated. He nodded. "Okay. I'll just get the young ones done today."

"Good idea. Wranglers are gonna be busy trying to prepare incase we can't get out very far tomorrow. Try to catch them first thing when they get back." He grabbed my face and kissed the top of my head. "I got some work to do but I'll be back later."

"Promise?" I asked as he started to walk away.

He stopped with his back to me. He dropped his dropped his head and turned around. Then he opened his mouth but then he closed it. "C'mere."

He mumbled, avoiding my eyes. I hurried to him and buried my face in his chest. I squeezed around him tight. "I'm gonna into town and get some paperwork done. And then I gotta stop at the reservation and take care of some horses. Then I'll be home. It might be after dark."

Please come home. I prayed. It's too cold for you to be out there.

*****

I picked up my phone and called Rip.

"Yeah." He answered.

"Hey. Is Kayce down there?" I asked nervously. "He said it could be after dark when he'd get back but I'm just a little worried."

"Nah. I haven't seen him since this morning." I heard Ryan and Colby in the back ground.

"Who Kayce?" Ryan's voice faintly said. Im assuming Rip nodded because he went on. "He's at the res. Monica's horses were stolen."

Then there was silence.

"Uh, yeah. He's not here. You want me to call him?" Rip stuttered on.

I swallowed hard. "Rip..." I closed my eyes and let out a sigh. "Did Ryan just say he's at Monica's?"

Rip cleared his throat. "Yes ma'am." He said.

I bit my tongue between my teeth. "Okay." I whispered. "Okay."

"Ya alright?" He asked hesitantly.

I had to think about it.

No. Not fucking really.

"Yeah. I'm good. Thanks, Rip." I hung up the phone and dialed Kayce's number.

It rang and rang and rang. No answer. Hell, he probably didn't have signal at the res.

Why didn't he just tell me they were Monica's horses? Not that that would've helped any but still. Why the hell is he helping her?

I paced around then called Hannah. No answer.

"Dammit." I cursed.

Then the power went out.

"Are you fucking kidding me..." I shook my head and looked outside for our wood pile. There was none. But I could still see a light on at the bunkhouse. If it gets too cold, I'll head down there.

My fire burned out quickly. It didn't take long for it to get too cold. The wind beat hard against the wooden house and soon I didn't know if I could stand it any longer.

Then Rip called.

"I'm coming to get ya. We just lost power and the wind is getting bad." Was all he said.

"Okay." I didn't argue. There was no reason. I was already freezing with layers on.

Soon Rip opened the door.

"How long have you been without power?" Then he looked to the fireplace. "You don't have any firewood?" He questioned.

I was already upset and frustrated so the questions put my on edge. "A couple hours. And no. Kayce was going to chop wood this morning but then he had to leave."

I swallowed hard. Leave to go to Monica's. I let out a shaky breath.

Rips face softened. "Grab your coat. C'mon."

I did so and then slipped on my boots.

The cold wind took the air from my chest as soon as we stepped outside. "Jesus, Mary, and Joesph." I mumbled as I got into the truck, shaking violently.

"It's bad." Rip put the truck in reserve and flew down the hill to the bunkhouse. I dreaded getting out again. I didn't know how he could see anything. It was a white out. I have had never seen anything like it.

He parked the truck and jumped out. I tried to push open my door but the wind was too strong. A few moments later, the door flung open, the piercing wind cutting my face and hands. I tucked my head down, trying to get the wind off my face. Rip reached in and grabbed me by the coat, pulling me out in one rough pull. My feet clumsily hit the ground and I staggered to walk. I had to squeezed my eyes shut. I reached back to find the truck but Rip wrapped his arm around my back and shoulders and trucked us to the door of the bunkhouse. The bunkhouse door flung open and smacked the cabinets behind it. We nearly fell in. Lloyd closed the door behind us.

I stood frozen, quite literally and figuratively. The fireplace crackled quietly in the background. A radio station buzzed and instead of the typically Texas Country music, it was a weather man stuttering along. When I opened my eyes, all the guys stared at me and Rip.

"Get that fire hotter. She's been out of power for a while and no fire. She's bout to freeze." Rip barked at the boys. Jake jumped up and grabbed some logs.

Rip touched my back and tried to move me. But I couldn't yet. I was still shaking. After a couple moments, I sighed.

If Kayce was here, we'd be at the cabin, curled up all warm and cozy in front of his fire place. Sipping a glass of bourbon or drinking a beer. Probably bare skinned.

My heart thumped harder.

That's probably what he's doing with her.

I stumbled to the fireplace. I wiped my face and leaned against the wall. "God, I miss Texas." I mumbled, rubbing my eyes.

**24**

---

They were all I could think about all night. I laid there in the bunk above Rip, tears streaming down my face. No cries or whimpers. Just pathetic tears.

There's no way they'll be in the same house all night and not have any intimate moments. They'll at least kiss. They have history. They could be making up right now. God, they could be making out right now.

I swallowed hard and put my hand over my mouth, trying to hush the cry that I was afraid would sneak out.

He knew it would be a snow storm tonight. He told me. Why would he even go over there? Am I dramatic to think that's messed up? Am I over thinking this? What the hell do I do when he comes back tomorrow? Maybe I should just pack my shit and leave, that way there's no awkward conversation or argument. I'll just leave and he can have her. They can find a new vet.

I don't wanna leave. Hot tears poured down even harder. I inhaled a small whimper on accident.

I didn't really care at this point. My throat hurt so bad from holding it in and I was getting a headache from it. My eyes ached and burned. I wanted to go back to the cabin and lay in our bed and cry into the cold, cold sheets. I didn't care if I froze to death in the cabin or on the drive up there. I really don't care.

I was too busy with my self pity thoughts, I didn't focus on keeping quiet. I didn't notice until under me Rip started to stir under me. Then he got up.

He rubbed his beard and sighed. "I'm really sorry you heard Ryan."

I rolled flat onto my back. "Why didn't you tell me?" I whispered, staring up at the ceiling, tears racing gravity down my temples.

He looked down,"I wanted you to hear it from Kayce."

"What do you think they're doing?" I asked. When he didn't answer, I turned my head to him. "I doubt he's sleeping on the couch and she's sleeping in the bed." My voice cracked.

Rip shook his head,"Don't put yourself there right now."

"Well I can't fucking think of anything else." My words were sharp and harsh. I was taking it out on him. "I'm sorry." I looked back up at the ceiling and started crying again, upset I just got mad at the man- who probably saved me from freezing to death- for absolutely no reason.

"Is there anything I can do?" He asked softly.

It wasn't a question I expected from him. And definitely not in a tone he used from often. The same voice he spoke to me with the night Kayce was shot.

I thought hard about the question. Can you lay here with me and pretend you're Kayce? No. That's wrong. I don't wanna give him the wrong idea.

Take me back to college? No. There's a blizzard outside. Go drinking at the bars? No, blizzard. Take me to the reservation so I can yell at him and ask why I'm not good enough? Blizzard.

I closed my eyes, "I don't even wanna see him." I whispered so softly.

"For how long?" Rip asked.

"I don't know." Here came the tears again. A small cry escaped my lips.

Rip grabbed my hand and squeezed. It was a comforting touch. Rub over my knuckles with your thumb like Kayce does. His hands were calloused and rough but they still didn't feel like Kayce's. "You're welcome to stay here for as long as you need. You're family whether you're with Kayce or not. We want you here." His gruffly voice was so quiet you almost couldn't hear it. But I heard enough of it.

I wiped my eyes with my free hand,"I don't know if I can stay." I squeezed his hand.

"I want you here, Ada."

The statement made me feel a different kind of way. I swallowed hard then sat up. Rip's face was dark in the dimmed bunkhouse but I could still see the emotion in his face. His somber face was mixed with something else. Maybe anger but I couldn't tell.

I pursed my lips together. What does he mean by that? My mind raced. I don't need this right now. I have too much going on as it is. Don't add something else to the mix, please.

"Rip..." I shook my head slowly.

He let go of my hand and put his hands on my knees. "You don't have to say anything. But I want you to know, that if he hurts you like this ever again," He clenched his jaw and exhaled deeply,"I won't be able to stand back and watch it happen."

Maybe my emotions were all over the place and I couldn't process what I was doing. Maybe I wanted to feel like some kind of connection because the one I had with Kayce was changing and being ripped away. Or maybe just because I wanted to.

I reached out and held the side of his face. My small hand against his scratchy beard. "You're a good man, Rip."

"If you think so, then I've done enough." His eyes looked longingly at me.

I sighed and leaned in. I kissed him gently on the cheek. "Thank you. I'm sorry I woke you up." I laid back down onto my side.

He shook his head. "You didn't wake me, darlin'. Jimmys snoring did." I giggled a little. Then he grinned a little. Neither of us could fully smile. "You wake me up if you need. You hear me?" His sternness rang out. I nodded. "You warm enough? Need another blanket or anything?"

I was cold. "A blanket would be nice." I whispered.

"Alright." He went to get one then brought it back shortly after. He draped it over me, then patted my thigh through the five layers of blankets and multiple layers of clothes. "Goodnight."

"Goodnight, Rip."

Then I finally closed my eyes and no tears drained from them. I let out a deep breath, and slept.

*****

"Why can't I go with?" I ruffled my eyebrows at Lloyd.

"Because it's -12 degrees with three feet of snow and ice. Just stay inside for right now. If it's not too bad, I'll come back and get ya." He grabbed his coat and slung it on.

"No you won't." I rolled my eyes and laid back dramatically onto the bunk. I heard Ryan chuckle then walk my way.

"All we're gonna do is check fence anyway. And you hate checking fences." He shook his head and stood beside my bed.

I stared at him. "I mean, yeah." I mumbled.

He smiled. "See. Stay in here and keep warm. We need our vet alive and ready to go incase something happens."

I waved them all off and said a silent prayer. Something I hadn't done in a long while. I prayed they stayed safe and warm and came home quick. I prayed the cattle were all okay and there was no damage anywhere. I prayed Kayce would come home and tell me he never even went to Monica's, that he stayed at the office in town.

But even God laughed at that prayer.

## 25

- - - - - - - - - - - - - - - - - - - - - - - - - - - - - - - - - - - - - - - - - - -

I spent the whole day a nervous wreck, waiting for everyone to come back. I made chili and cornbread. Sweet cornbread. I didn't like it but it's what the boys liked so that's how I made it. I wanted to make a pie but there wasn't any fruit or canned pie filling so I had to pass on that.

Everybody was back before dark, and that's how I knew how bad it was outside. It was rare for us to be done before eight or nine on any normal day. So when they all trudged in at four thirty, I got worried.

"Smells good in here." Lloyd smiled as he walked in the door behind Colby.

I grinned,"I figured y'all would be hungry."

"As long as it's warm." Colby slipped off his boots and went straight for the stove.

The others came in slowly behind them. Ryan's nose was bright red and then blue at the end when he pulled down his bandana.

I grabbed a cloth and ran it under warm water than rang it out.

He flopped onto the couch and took his hat off.

"Put this on your nose," I asked,"You feeling okay?" I handed him the rag.

He took it and did as he was told. His hands were bruised almost but I didn't look too close. He shook his head a little. "Just check on Rip." He was short of breath and shivering.

He hadn't came inside yet. But I looked around. "Where is he?" I looked at Lloyd now.

"He-"

The door opened and slammed shut as Rip stumbled in. I hurried to him. "What's wrong?" I asked, trying to guide him to the fireplace. I was taken aback by how he looked. His cheek was red and swollen and his bottom lip looked blue and black.

What's wrong? Seriously, Ada? It's negative degrees and a blizzard and you asked this man what's wrong.

He didn't give me a smart ass answer like I expected from him. He looked down at me and pulled his gloves off. I bit my tongue and dreadfully looked down at them. I already knew what I was about to see.

Both were blood red. But on his right hand, from his knuckles to his finger tips, a pale blue. And then the tip of his ring finger and almost all of his pinky was dark blue. The tip of his middle finger was black. That was what I expected.

I didn't expect the bloodied knuckles that were busted open. That didn't look like frostbite.

I looked at Ryan was also had bruised hands.

"What did you two do?" I whispered, before hurrying to grab whatever I could find. There wasn't much I could do or that I knew how to do. I planned to treat him as I treated an animals wounds. I didn't know what else to do.

I ran to the washroom and turned on the sink. The water was ice cold for several minutes. It slowly started to get warm. I called for him to come in.

Rip stepped into the washroom.

"Put your hands under that." I instructed while I reached in to turn the shower on.

"It's cold." He took his hands away and tried to turn the hot water up.

I quickly turned it back to where it was. "No it's not. You just can't tell." I sifted through the cabinets, looking for cotton balls and ace bandages. His skin was definitely going to start peeling or blistering soon if he didn't get warm. "Take off your coat, you're going to start sweating and that's gonna make it worse." When I didn't hear him take it off, I just assumed he was being stubborn. I rolled my eyes.

I felt the shower. It was finally just warm enough for him.

"Alright. At least half an hour in there." He kicked off his boots and then I heard him mess with his belt. I turned around to leave. But then I didn't hear anything more. I closed my eyes and pressed my lips together. "Can you get it?" I asked, hesitant at first.

"No. I can't feel my fucking hands and it's all frozen."

"Okay." It came out as a whisper. I turned back around. I reached up and unbuttoned his shirt. I tried not to think about anything other than just helping him. "I've never seen busted knuckles from frost bite." I muttered. He didn't say anything. "Or a fat lip." I looked up at him. He was staring down at me. I quickly looked away and back to the buttons. I pushed the shirt over his shoulders and he turned to help me pull it down. It was fine until it met his skin below the short sleeve. It held tight to his skin. "Oh." I swallowed hard. "Um. Hang on." I reached for my phone and dialed Hannah's number.

She picked up on the second ring. "Hey, I've been trying to call you. Are you okay?"

"Yeah I'm fine, they got the generator dug out and working this morning so we've got power. You guys okay?" I stared at Rips red skin.

"Yeah, we're staying at the clinic."

"I got a question." I asked immediately after.

"Shoot."

"How familiar are you with frostbite?" I chewed on my nails.

It was silent for a moment. "Ada, you know more about it than I do. Um, is it a horse or cattle? I can go ask Dad." I heard her pacing in the background.

"It's Rip."

"Oh. Okay." Her voice sounded shocked, as expected. "I know a little. How bad is it?"

"His shirt is stuck to his skin." I put my hand to my forehead and looked closer. Then I pulled on the shirt some.

"Does it hurt?" She asked.

I tugged harder and it came down an inch or so with a tearing sound.

"Fuck." He cussed and gritted his teeth.

I let go of the shirt immediately. "Yeah I think so." I told Hannah.

"Honestly, all you can do is get a warm rag and try to unthaw it. I would treat it like you would take clothes off a burn, you know? Don't rub or anything, just get it wet and pull it off."

I nodded. "That's what I was thinking. Believe it or not, I've never had to treat frostbite." I mumbled, grabbing another rag and running it under the water.

"I'm surprised, Texas." She teased on the other end.

"Thanks, Han." I smiled even though she couldn't see me.

"You're welcome, babe." I could hear her smiling too.

I looked up at Rip after we hung up the phone. "I have no idea what I'm doing." I told him.

He opened his mouth then closed it. "You'll do fine." He nodded once.

I could tell he was weary about it and I don't blame him. I was about to be peeling this shirt off and just praying I didn't take the skin with.

Every time I placed the warm rag on the shirt, it got cold within seconds. By the time I turned around and warmed the cloth back up, the shirt froze back to his skin.

"Hey Lloyd?" I hollered out.

"Yeah." He came in fast. "What's wrong?"

"I need your help." I sighed, "His shirt is stuck to his skin and I can't keep it warm and damp long enough to peel it off."

Rip, who was clearly over all this, became antsy. "Let me just get in the shower with it." He argued.

"No." I repeated for the millionth time.

"Why not?" He grunted.

"Because you'll try to pull it off and it's gonna hurt your skin even worse than it already is. Just be patient." I gave the rag to Lloyd who warmed it up under the skin.

We kept rotating the warm rags and I was soon able to slowly pull the sleeves down. Rip stared straight ahead. He didn't flinch or complain or anything. But I knew it had to be hurting.

Now we just had the t shirt.

"Is that frozen too?" I asked, putting my hand on his chest.

He nodded.

I ruffled my brows. "Turn around." He did so. "I have a hard time believing this is just from the cold." I started in again and grabbed a rag from Lloyd, I started on Rips back.

"That's because it's not." Lloyd spoke up finally.

"Lloyd." Rip tried to cut him off.

I looked at Lloyd. "What happened?"

He gave it to me straight. "Kayce came back. Rip told him not to go near you. They got mad and they fought. Both of them being fucking idiots."

"He's here?" I snapped my head up to Rip. "What, you just weren't going to say anything?" My blood boiled. I grabbed a pair of scissors and stepped behind him. I started to cut through his T-shirt.

Rip turned towards me some, looking over his shoulder,"You said you didn't want to see him."

"I wouldn't argue with her right now." Lloyd mumbled and looked back to the sink, warming up the rags.

I ignored him. "I was just upset, I didn't actually mean it. And it would've been nice to at least know he made it home. And I also didn't say to beat the snot out of each other. Quit moving." I mumbled and tossed the scissors into the drawer and slammed it closed. He tried to face me again. I had ahold of his shirt and it tore against his skin as he turned. "Careful." I winced, imaging the pain as it pulled off a small layer of skin. He acted as if it didn't bother him.

"You say jump and I don't ask how high. I just jump." His eyes narrowed down at me and his chest moved up and down heavily. "Do you understand?"

Although he was nearly frozen, I could feel the heat coming off of his body. He was pissed to say the least. I looked back at Lloyd. He watched us both carefully. He gave me a look. And I knew it meant that there wasn't anything I could say to help right now. There was no use in arguing.

"Yeah, I understand." I nodded and patted his chest. I don't like it though. "Now turn around, we're almost done."

*****

"Is he alright?" Ryan asked as soon as I stepped out of the washroom. His nose was still red but the blue was now gone.

I nodded,"Yeah, it's just gonna take a while for him to warm back up. His shirt froze to his skin." I sat down on the couch beside him with a blank stare. I didn't know what to do now. I looked at Ryan's hands. "I know why Rips all busted up. What about you?" I asked him.

He sighed and rubbed his forehead. "Somebody had to split them up. It's so slick out that they only got a few punches in before they hit the ground and fell through that ice. They fucking know that pond is there."

"Wait a minute," I tried playing this out in my head,"He didn't mention the pond-" I opened my mouth. Then closed it. Then opened again. "They got in a fight? On top of the frozen pond? And then fell through?" I stood up.

Ryan nodded. "I'll be surprised if they're not sick."

"What about Kayce, is he hurt bad?" I ran up to grab my coat and boots.

"Ada-" Lloyd jumped up and stopped me. "You can't go out there. It's dropped ten degrees since we've came in and it's a blizzard again. Weatherman said it's gonna be worse tonight then it was last night. You won't even be able to make it to the truck."

I stared at him, tears started to whelm up in my eyes. There was so many arguments I could make but none were going to lead me to getting out of here. It was useless and they were probably right. "I really think someone should check on him." I bit down on my lip, trying to keep the tears in.

"He was a navy seal. He's tough, kid. He's gonna be fine." Lloyd patted my shoulder.

I know he is but he's alone.

I nodded and went back to the couch. I pulled my legs up to my chest under a small blanket in front of the fire that wasn't providing much warmth. It wasn't long before Rip got out of the shower. He came over and sat down beside me.

"I shouldn't have started-"

I stopped him. "For someone who preaches about no fighting, you sure do fight a lot." I clenched my teeth together and stared at his dark eyes.

His eyes wondered away from me. "I know. But this was different."

"I appreciate you looking out for me," I swallowed hard, trying to stay calm and not throw a fit. He's going to take me seriously if I'm not acting like a fool. "But I'm a big girl. And if he would've walked through that door and I didn't want to see him, he would've left one way or the other."

He started to say something, but then stopped. "You remember when I brought you back to the cabin after we put Kayce in the helicopter?"

Do I remember? Yeah, it was the worst night of my life.

"Yeah." I whispered.

"Hannah got there, and I let go of you. And you said don't leave me alone again. And I can't get that out of my head." His face drooped. "I didn't know if you really wanted to see him or not. But he was coming here and hell, that's what he should've done. But if you didn't want to see him, I wasn't leaving you alone again."

He put his hand on my shoulder. The tears came back and I brushed them away quickly.

"I wish you would've found a way other than fighting over a frozen pond." I teased, as the tears fell.

"Well-"

The bunkhouse door opened with a loud crash. Everyone jumped and looked in the direction. The man in doorway was covered in snow and ice. What little skin I could see, was bright red. Kayce stumbled around then looked directly at me. Then at Rip, who still had his hand casually resting on my shoulder.

"You better fucking move your hands." Kayce growled and limped towards Rip, snow falling from him as he did so.

Not again. "Kayce, wait-" I stood up from the couch.

Rip stood up too. "Calm down-" Kayce fisted connected to Rips jaw.

"Hey! That's enough!" Lloyd yelled as Ryan jumped off his bed and came running to us.

Rip returned some blows.

Colby ran up and grabbed me, pulling me out of the way. Between Jimmy, Jake, and Ryan, they got them split apart.

"I'm gone for one fucking night!" Kayce yelled at Rip, fighting against Jimmy and Ryan.

I shook at the sound of him yelling. I had heard him yell before whether it was in the pastures or the times with Jake but this was different. It was filled with hate. It wasn't something I had heard before from him and I never wanted to again.

"Yeah, and where were you? You left her at that damn cabin with no firewood and the power went out. She was gonna fucking freeze to death up there!" Rip yelled back around Jake.

"So you had to come in and save her, huh?! Just like you did with Monica!" Kayce pushed Ryan and Jimmy off him but he stayed at a stand still. His chest rising and falling fast. His fists were in balls at his side and his face was red. His temple had a small cut on it and his cheek was swelling.

"You never answered my question." Rip gritted through his teeth.

Jake shook his head at Rip. "This isn't the place for this." I heard him mumble.

Kayce glanced over at me and I nearly broke right then. Tears that were already in my eyes started pouring out. Colby was the only thing keeping me from collapsing onto the floor.

"I was at Monica's-" His voice was deep and raspy. I squeezed my eyes shut. No. Don't do this to me. Not after everything we've been through. "But it wasn't like that. It was work, Ada. I swear. Just let me explain." He started towards me and Colby.

"No." I choked out the words. He froze in his steps. "Just... please." I swallowed hard and pulled myself together. "Leave me alone." I hurried towards the wash room and closed the door behind me. There was more yelling and arguing but I tried to tone it out. I turned on the shower and undressed.

Then I sat in the bottom of the shower and cried as if I hadn't been crying for two days already.

# 26

----------------------------------------------------------------

It was cliche for it to rain today. Middle of winter in Montana, and it rained, not snowed. Anyone you spoke to today commented on it.

"I ain't seen this in the 60 years I've lived here."

"This'll make a muddy mess for sure."

"I bet them cattle are hating this."

"It's gonna tear up everyone's pastures even worse than they already are."

If I heard one more comment about the rain, I would pray for a flood.

Though, to be honest, it already came a flood. When it rained, it poured. And lord was it pouring.

*****

I stared down at the navy blue dress that sat on my legs. The small white polka dots bunched together and I started to count them. Anything to keep my mind off of what was happening. The preachers voice made that hard. He had a strong, loud sermon to give about life and death, past and present, and moving on.

"Though my flesh and my heart may fail, but God is the strength of my heart and my portion forever..."

His words rang out as he quoted from what I think is from the book of Psalm. I didn't like that this is the verse he chose. There were many more that would be better suited in our position here. Because in fact, science is what failed Dr Stone. Man failed Dr Stone. His heart and his flesh was healthy at one time and could have stayed that way, if only modern medicine persisted. But cancer was a devil that had yet to be killed.

Hannah sniffled beside me again. "Why did your dad want a Methodist preacher if he was catholic?" I leaned over and playfully whispered in her ear. "We're gonna be here until dark."

A little smile broke through on her face through the tears. She leaned over at me,"He didn't. But the priest said he started burning when he walked in the same room as us." Her voice was raspy and broken.

My jaw dropped a little and I lightly slapped her arm. She may have lost her father, but her sense of humor was still there. She grinned a little but it quickly turned into a contorted frown with tears furiously pouring out. I gave her a sad look, and reached around, grabbing her shoulder and pulling her towards me. She dropped her head down low onto my shoulder, her blonde hair falling. I felt her body become weak.

Ryan quickly looked over at me, noticing the change in position. I gave him the same look I gave Hannah. His eyes were cloudy as well, seeing his best friend in so much pain. Hannah audibly sobbed and I squeezed her tighter, as the preacher continued, trying to ignore and push through the poor daughters cries.

The preacher seemed to cut his sermon short when he realized the toll it was taking on us all. He dismissed us by rows, and since we were in the front, we were last. I was still holding Hannah and kept an eye out for when we needed to stand. But I caught a glimpse of a familiar face starting to stand in the one of the first rows that left.

Kayce.

I turned my head quickly to see if I was imaging it. His broad shoulders were covered with the grey suit jacket. It looked ironed but I knew he wasn't the one who had done it. He had asked for my help one before and when I tried to show him, there was no hope.

"It's not working." He mumbled from the ironing board. The iron made a swishing sound as he pressed harder.

I giggled and rolled my eyes as I put on the earrings Kayce had given me last night for what he called an "early Christmas gift", even though it was October. But I didn't mind. They were beautiful, small, gold hoops. Something I had been eyeing for months now. "Honey, I don't care to do it." I walked up behind him, placing my hand on his lower back.

"But what if you're not here?" He sat the iron down and turned around to me.

It took me by surprise. "Well..." I shrugged and exhaled deeply,"I don't know. But I didn't plan on going no where." My words were sharper than I intended and sounded a little harsh.

Kayce's hair light brown hair was pushed back behind his ears and his beard was freshly trimmed. He smelled like his soap. The smell always filled the entire house when he got out of the shower. He ran a hand across his bare chest, rubbing his shoulder. He had been doing this often. I assumed it was a pull muscle or ache. "I didn't mean it like that. Just..." he sighed, shook his head, then dropped his hand back to his side,"If you're not here at the cabin, or you're on a trip, or something-"

"I can iron it before I leave. Or you can call Beth." I patted his chest, and stretched up to peck his cheek.

He turned his face so his lips would greet mine. I smiled into it. He pulled me in close to him by my hips. "Don't go anywhere." He mumbled against my lips. It wasn't the teasing, playful Kayce I was use to.

Confused, I pulled back to get a clearer look on his face. "I'm not, baby."

Likely Beth ironed it. His hair was a little longer now and pushed behind his ears under that same damn cowboy hat. The nice one. The one he wore on our first date. His beard was cleaner kept and his mustache was trimmed. I loved when he spent the extra time to maintain it. It wasn't always practical and I knew that, but admired it still. He must have sensed I was watching because he met my eyes. He stopped were he was, and his pale lips parted slightly. My eyes teared up. I didn't want to see him but I needed to see him. John stood behind him and realized what he saw. He touch his shoulder, causing Kayce to come back to realization. Kayce moved forward but looked out to me multiple more times over his shoulder.

It had been almost a year, though it felt longer than that, since I went back to Texas. I returned to school in Wyoming but had to make up for lost time. It was good to be with Hannah again. But in the past six months, a lot had changed. Dr Stone, although he out lived longer than every doctor said he would, was finally getting worse. They stopped chemo and radiation, it wasn't doing any good. She wanted to spend as much time with him as possible, and I didn't blame her. The biggest problem at hand was that when Dr Stone passed, there wouldn't be a licensed veterinarian at the clinic. The clinic would have to close. Hannah and I had a long discussion about how to go about this. We both couldn't stay in school. Someone had to be at the clinic to run things. Our final decision was finalized when we were told Dr Stone didn't have more than six months left, and this time we could tell that was true. Hannah had less classes to complete than myself, and to be honest, she was smarter and more determined. She could pack her schedule full plus some and passed everything. She had a year left of classes to finish in six months. Her graduation was suppose to be this week.

I spent every day here in Montana for the last month trying to avoid anyone who knew me. At first I was able to make the trip up from Texas every couple of weeks to keep things on track but it was busy season and that wasn't possible recently. It was brutal being here and quite honesty I hated it. Everything reminded me of Kayce. I saw Ryan nearly every over day but he swore not to tell Kayce I was back. By the reaction I saw from Kayce, Ryan didn't break his promise.

The ride to the cemetery was painful. Hannah was nearly incoherent. Ryan and I almost carried her to the tent where the small graveside service would be held. It only lasted a few minutes before most rushed off and through the rain.

Hannah wanted to leave immediately so Ryan took her home.

"I'll come back and get you. Just text me when everything is finished." He patted my shoulder as he nearly carried Hannah away. So I sat alone as three men silently worked on the finishing touches. I never knew what happened when everyone left the cemetery but I was about to find out.

One man reopened the casket and placed a white sheet over the frail body that use to a father and a veterinarian. Then he closed it back and started to seal the casket.

There was movement beside me. I looked up at the man who stood with drops of rain dripping from the brim of his hat. He sat down slowly in the folding green chair next to me. Then he put his arm around my shoulders and pulled me in just like I did to Hannah only an hour ago. I sniffled and my lip quivered. "I'm tired, Kayce." My voiced cracked as hot tears streamed down my cheeks, red from the bitter cold wind.

"I know." His rough hand rubbed up and down my bicep to my shoulder. A comforting gesture. I reluctantly leaned into him, weak and exhausted. My body shivered as I cried and fell to his chest. His arms grasped around me. My hands pushed onto his chest. I had no energy to even raise them to around his neck, nor did I want to. I didn't want him to know I would let him back in. "I know." He whispered and turned his head to rest his chin on the top of my head. He pressed his lips to my hair gently.

It made me wonder what he knew. Did he know I wasn't letting him back in? That I was just hurting and tired and wanted some point of normalcy again. That being in his arms and time spent with him felt normal. Or are these just meaningless words of comfort? Sometimes we say what we're suppose to say because we've been told it helps.

I didn't ask.

"Is it over?" I asked, sobbing more. I didn't even know what I was referring to. I guess it was the funeral and the stress of taking care of Dr Stone and Hannah and the clinic all at once.

"Yeah, it's over." He said softly, his finger tips pressing against my rib cage. His other hand buried into my hair, holding me to him. It felt nice. Normal.

Time passed slowly as my cries slowly stopped. The rain was still coming down in waves. Hard and loud, then letting up some but never fully stopping. The wind occasionally blowing caused the droplets to fly under into the tent. The temperature dropped some and the cold breeze made my arms and face tingle before the goosebumps formed.

Kayce had relaxed some, but still held me tight to him. I needed him to let go but I didn't want that.

"I want you to come home." He whispered. I barely made out the words through the constant pounding of the rain on the tent.

"This isn't the time-" I shook my head some. My fore head rested on his chest. The fabric of his button down shirt smell familiar. Normal. The same laundry soap my clothes were washed in. He use to buy the five gallon bucket of Arm & Hammer powder detergent. Sure, it cleaned the clothes but they didn't smell like the lavender Mrs. Meyers and Downy I was use to. I bought my typical laundry supplies a short month or so after I moved in and Kayce got to come home from the hospital. Even the first time after I washed the bedding and his clothes in it, he noticed.

"What detergent did you use?" He asked, as he pulled on a t-shirt. He put the shirt to his nose.

My face flushed. I didn't want him to think I was overtaking his home but I couldn't take the dry, stiff laundry any longer. "Uh, it's Mrs. Meyers." I said over my shoulder as I combed through my wet hair in front of the steamy bathroom mirror.

"Mrs. what?" His face showed a confused expression and it made me giggle.

"Meyers. It's just what I normally use. I can go back to the other-" He walked over and leaned against the door frame of the bathroom, looking down at me. "What?" I asked, looking up at him.

He grinned a little, and pushed my wet hair over my shoulder as he does often. "I like it." He leaned down and pressed his lips onto my temple, then started to walk back to where he was.

"Are you sure?" My words were quiet and nervous.

He grabbed his belt that was hanging on the door knob of the bedroom door. "Yeah." He nodded. He looked down and threaded the leather strap through the belt loops of his jeans.

I stepped out of the bathroom, and leaned against the door frame myself now. "I don't want you to think I'm trying to-" I lost the words. "You know." I sighed.

He looked up through the hair that fell in front of his face. He quickly pushed it back out of his face, shook his head, and looped the end tip of the belt through the frame of the buckle. He pulled it back the opposite way then pierced one of the punch holes with the prong, and laced it through the belt loop again.

I watched him quietly.

"You don't want me to think what, baby?" He asked, a little more concerned now. He pulled his boots on then walked back to me. "Alright, what's wrong?" He took my face in his hands, forcing me to meet his eyes.

"I don't want you to think I'm trying to change everything or take over or-"

He pushed his lips onto mine suddenly. My words were silenced and I kissed him back gently. He slowly pulled away, his beard grazing my skin. "You can change whatever you want, darlin'. This is your home, too. It always will be."

Kayce let go of me suddenly, snapping me out of my memory. "You just left, Ada." He ruffled his brows and looked down at my teary eyes. "You didn't even want to try to make it work-"

"You slept with Monica." My tears dried up as anger grew into my mind.

He stood up, abruptly. "Don't say it like that. I didn't fucking sleep with her-"

I jumped up too now,"But you made out with her!"

"It didn't mean anything!" He stepped close to me, trying to defend himself.

"It doesn't matter! You laid in bed with her all night while I was at the cabin, waiting for you until Rip came and got me so I didn't fucking freeze to death!" I nearly screamed at him, I was inches from him. The tears started up again but not for Dr. Stone, for my own selfish heart.

His voice pushed through the sound of the rain. "Because he always fuck-ing saves you-!"

"Because he gave a damn about me!" I yelled back, as the wind blew harder. Rain drops hit my face and mixed in with the tears. "He fucking cared! And you didn't!"

"I did, goddamn it! I still do!" Kayce yelled over my next sentence.

Our bitterness overlapped, and I pushed against his chest. "No! You didn't care, Kayce! 'Cause if you did you wouldn't have done this! You wouldn't have ruined everything! I fell in love with you and you ruined everything just like everyone said you would!" The words fell from my mouth without a choice. They flew from my tongue like an ugly buzzard down to pick up roadkill. It was disgusting and I immediately regretted it. I felt my shoulders curling inward and my body becoming weak. I wanted to lay down and disappear.

I couldn't see his face through my tears or the rain becoming heavier and blowing into the tent even more, soaking us both. I was glad I couldn't. I didn't want to know how I made him feel. I always put everyone's opinions and thoughts about Kayce out of my mind. I didn't even know where the comment came from, but it was hateful and ugly.

And it didn't mean anything.

-------------------------------------------------------------------

## 27

"So you two did slept together?" I sniffled, and wiped my cheek with the back of my hand. My cheeks felt warm and I knew they were bright red from the stress and pain I was feeling.

Monica hung her head, and looked down at her lap. She was so pretty sitting across the room from me on her couch. Her long hair cascaded across her slender frame. It was no wonder Kayce was attracted to her.

"I wouldn't say it like that. He was just laid there with me. And we made out but then he came back in here." She mumbled, her voice cracking some. She was hurting, too.

More tears ran down my face. "Why?" I asked.

"I don't know. It was stupid-" She shook her head. "I thought maybe I could guilt him back into- into loving me." She sniffled too.

"Guilt him?" I stood up. "What did you say-" I started to raise my voice but quickly stopped. I wanted to hear this from him. "Never mind. Thanks for being honest with me, Monica." I went for the door.

"Wait, Ada-" She stood up, tears streaming down her high cheek bones,"I'm really sorry. I didn't know how much he loved you-"

I cut her off. I didn't want to hear anymore. "I'm sorry, too. I know you've been through a lot." I tried to give a small smile and wiped my face as I pushed open the door.

It was dark that night. No moon in the sky and very few stars. It was brutally cold but I didn't want to go back to the cabin. So I sat in the barn. In a stall on hay covered concrete. The horses in the other stalls didn't move much. They were cold too.

The sound of shuffling coming through the barn filled my ears.

"You're gonna freeze." Rip pushed the door open.

I didn't say anything or even look up at him. "I don't even care." My tired voice struggled to push the words out.

He sighed and walked over. He sat down beside me with a grunt. "What'd Monica say?"

"What makes you think I talked to her?" I tried fake my way through it.

He huffed and shook his head. "If you went to Hannah or the clinic, you would've just stayed there for the night. If you went to the bar, you would've called me to come get you. And it's too cold for you to go anywhere else."

I pulled my knees to my chest and wrapped my arms around them. I rested my chin on my knee. "Same thing he said. That her horses were stolen and he found 'em and by the time he got back it was a white out so she had him go inside and then they made out but she swears it was nothing more. She did say that she guilted him into everything."

"You can't guilt someone into cheating." He mumbled in a hateful tone.

"I don't know," I sighed loudly. "I don't even know if I can call it that."

"Call it what you want, but it's wrong, Ada. What he did was wrong." He grumbled.

I stared at the wood panels in the stall. One specific one had multiple knots in it. I traced them with my eyes.

I didn't say anything back to him. I knew it was wrong. I just didn't know what to do now.

We sat in silence for a while until he slowly got up. "You coming with?" He asked, dusting his jeans off.

"Maybe later. I need to think some more." There was no way I would go into that bunkhouse right now. I had a splotchy face and smeared mascara. They would pity me and I wasn't in the mood for that.

"Alright. You know where I'll be if you need me." He started for the door.

"Rip?" I said. He turned around and stared down at me. "Thank you. For just being here." I swallowed hard.

"I'm always going to be here for you. No matter what." He let the words linger in the air. I knew what it meant. "Goodnight, Ada."

"Goodnight." I whispered.

It wasn't but ten minutes later when I heard to familiar shuffling sound again.

But this time a cowboy peeked over the stall and froze when he saw me. "Why are you out in the cold, babe? You're gonna get sick." Kayce disappeared for a moment then came back with an Aztec print blanket.

He hurried into the stall and kneeled down in front of me. I looked at his perfect imperfect face. He focused on draping the blanket around me and I stared at his eyes. He met my stare.

"How do I fix this?" He whispered with so much pain in his voice.

"She said she guilted you into it. What did she say to you?" My straining words were barely loud enough to hear.

But he heard me.

He sighed and sat up against the wall next to me. On the opposite side that Rip had just been not long ago.

"I didn't even think she would talk to me but she kept bringing up our marriage. And everything I did wrong and I ruined it all and how it was my fault we divorced and-" I stared at his somber face. He regretted it. I could tell. But what was done was already done. He took his hat off and tossed it on the ground in front of us. He ran a hand through his hair. "I was a terrible husband, Ada. And I never apologized to her. So I sat down with her and finally did. And she started crying and I felt awful so I- I held her for a while. And I should've known she was playing me because she started kissing me after and I- I didn't stop her."

I didn't even have the energy to wipe away my tears. I didn't have the energy to fight or argue or even live. I wanted it to be done. I never wanted to talk about it again.

"You did ruin everything." I mumbled through the slow falling tears.

*****

I told him I was going to stay at the bunkhouse that night. And I planned on it after I went for a drive to clear my head. But I kept driving until I was crossing the Colorado state line by the time he started work the next morning.

# 28

- - - - - - - - - - - - - - - - - - - - - - - - - - - - - - - - - - - - - - - - -

"I can't leave you here." Kayce said in an exhausted voice. Drops of water dripped down off his dark hat and soaked his grey suit jacket.

I hastily sat back down in the small white folding chair, facing to where a casket once was just a short time ago. Not even an hour ago. I sighed loudly and dried the water from my face as best I could without smudging my make up as if that would've helped. It was likely I had smears of black mascara and patchy blush. "Ryan said he can come back and get me." I stared straight ahead, avoiding his kind eyes.

"Well, he's not here and I gotta get back to the ranch. And I ain't leaving you by yourself here." He shook his head, and I heard him walking away. The squishing of mud under his boots stopped for a moment and paused, as if he realized I wasn't following. He trudged back to me and knelt down in front of my little white chair. He narrowed his dark eyes and sighed a breath that sounded like it held a thousand pounds. He was frustrated with me and he was exhausted, probably from work or family or something between the two. I had heard this sigh many times before and that's what it always meant. It happened when Kayce was too drained to even entertain an argument. He was going to tell it how it was, and I would listen. But not this time. I was going to be tough and stay strong. "I don't give a damn how mad you are, or that you still hate me. But I'm not leaving you alone right now." The gravelly tone in which he spoke gave off that rough demeanor that made me remember one of the reasons why I had found him so attractive. The sternness and intensity made me giddy at one time, and that hadn't changed, because I ached to do as he said. I wanted to please him and make things easier for him because he does so much for everyone but himself.

But the image of him with Monica that I had created in my mind long ago floated by me. And I couldn't break from that picture.

Not this time. I repeated in my head. I stayed still, ready to throw my tantrum if needed. I wasn't going with him. I knew what that would do. "Ada, if I have to carry you to my truck, fightin' and screamin' I will. Please don't make me do that." He blinked slowly,"Just let me drive you home before it starts storming again." His chest fell slowly now as he breathed deeply. I heard his exhales over the rain. His eyes were dark and dreary and falling half shut. When's the last time this poor man slept?

I gritted my teeth. I can't. I bit my tongue. Don't do it. I told myself. I took my eyes from him and stared forward again.

He let out another one of those heavy sighs and stood up from his one knee. His tall figure sat down in the chair beside me. "I guess we'll ride out this storm together." He cleared his throat. "That'll be a first." He looked down at me.

The comment just pissed me off. He wasn't talking about a thunderstorm or snow storm. He meant our storm. The storm he caused. I opened my mouth to argue then stopped.

He knew me too well and that I would have to say something back.

"I'm only letting you take me home so I don't have to sit here with you any longer." I stood up and stomped away.

I stepped up into the truck and he shut the door behind me. The truck smelled the same as it use to and gave me nostalgia from the dates we had or errands we had to run together. I missed those times. I curled up in his passenger seat and stared out the window as the blue mountains and muddy pastures flashed by us. He didn't say a word. He didn't turn on the radio. He just drove. And it was peaceful. Comfortable. Safe. My eyelids kept dipping down and as much as I forced them open again, they won. They fell shut. The tap tap of the rain on the wind shield made a relaxing tune that put me in a sudden sleep.

When I opened my eyes, the truck was shut off, sitting in front of his cabin. The front porch swing swaying the in wind and the heavy rain. But I was alone in the truck. I swallowed hard. Of course he would do this. I couldn't blame him for trying.

There was a break in the rain and I pushed open the truck door, then hurried to the front porch. I shivered and twisted the door handle to let myself in the cabin. I froze as I stared around the place. It looked identical as it was before. I walked slowly to the kitchen. My heart raced and my chest hurt when I saw a note on the island.

Fixing fence. Be back in a little bit. There's still some of your clothes in the closet if you want to change or shower. This is still your home.

My jaw quivered as I read the last line. The truck keys sat by the note though. I could leave if I wanted to. I grabbed the metal truck keys and gripped them tightly as if they would fly away while the tears streamed down my face.

But then I put them down.

I pulled myself together and found my way into the room we spent so many nights together in. The closet to the right of the doorway once held almost all of my clothes and very few of his. I pushed the door open and saw that it looked bared now over than his jeans and button downs. A couple old sweatshirts and my jeans were still hanging up. I must have overlooked them when I left in a hurry.

A little past the closet was the bathroom where I had gotten ready every morning. My finger tips flicked the light switch on. The light filled the bathroom and hummed for a moment before going silent again. I glared at the stone floor shower. I didn't want to be in that shower ever again. Not without him.

It's strange the little things you miss in a person. There were countless gestures I missed about Kayce, but in the moment I missed his ability to make me forget. It didn't matter what happened on the ranch or at clinic that day, he would be able to make it all go away just with his touch.

I sniffled and stared at the front porch step between my feet. I felt numb and that I had failed. I felt like a failure.

The creak of the screen door drew my attention away from my self pity filled thoughts. I glanced over my shoulder as if I didn't already know who it was. Kayce's boots thumped against the wooden slats as he came closer. He sat down beside me and draped his arm around my shoulders.

"Bad day?" He asked, rubbing my arm and keeping me tight to him.

I nodded. "I lost a colt." I wiped my nose on the sleeve of my scrub jacket. "I shouldn't have. It was a stupid mistake." My voice cracked and the words barely made sense.

"Hey..." he gently hushed me as I fell into his chest. "You can't prevent something that was bound to happen in nature." He softly spoke in my ear as he wrapped his other arm around me. "You hear me?" He asked.

"But it still hurts like hell." I looked up at him.

His calloused hand held my jaw. "It's suppose to, baby. It makes you stronger. A better vet."

"I'm not even a vet. I couldn't even finish school. I can't do this." My tears fell one after another.

The wind blew a piece of my dark hair into my face. He pushed in back and leaned in closer. "You are a vet. A damn good vet. You don't need a piece of paper that tells that." He rested his forehead against mine. "There's nothing I can tell you to help with this, huh?"

I shook my head. "Im sorry."

"Don't be." His soft lips pressed gently against mine. Everything in me relaxed. I fell into him and kissed him again. His hands held my face as he pulled away. "I'll get you a shower going and start dinner."

I cracked a tiny smile. "You don't have to cook, Kayce." I tried to put it as nicely as possible, but him fixing dinner was not going to help anything in anyway.

He chuckled and stood up from the steps,"I'll go see what Gator fixed and bring you back some. How about that?" He held out his hand and helped me up.

I blinked the memory away. It had been nice to step into a hot shower with your clothes laid out and a warm towel by the sink. He had put a shower bomb in the bottom of the shower even though months before he had no idea what it was.

But that wasn't happening now. I was standing on a cold tile floor all alone.

An involuntary sigh escaped my lips as I stripped down my clothes. I reached in and turned the hot water on then wash the tears and make up off. It was nice to warm up under the hot water. I grabbed a towel and patted myself dry. As I stepped out of the shower, my eyes hung onto the floor in the far right corner of the room. Where I laid and sobbed when I thought I lost Kayce. It gave me chills. Back then, I thought I loved him. And I did but not near as much as I soon would after that. Not as much as I do now. I pushed past the dreaded feeling and changed into dry jeans, panties, socks, a sports bra and a raggedy old Texas LongHorns sweatshirt. I had left quite a few things here.

I briskly walked past our bed. I couldn't even look at it and I sure as hell didn't want to think about it.

I made myself a cup of coffee in the kitchen. The bitter scent started to fill the cabin. I took a mug full of the hot liquid and curled up on the couch in front of the dry fireplace. Then I waited.

Waited for him to come home, I guess. What else was there to wait for? I didn't know what I would do or say when he got here. But I wanted him here. Again, I found myself simply wanting him around.

It felt empty without him. Cold.

A few painfully quiet hours or so passed, until the front door squeaked open then closed. My breath caught in my throat. Here we go. I looked over my shoulder at him.

"Hey." Kayce said with a breathy voice. His clothes were dripping wet with tiny icicles that clung to the bridge of his hat and the crevices of his coat. The temperature most have drop drastically. His face was pale besides the tip of his nose which was red and blistered. His lips were turning blue.

"My God." I jumped up quickly. "You couldn't find a tree to stay dry under or something." I hurried to him but suddenly had to stop myself from grabbing his face or taking him coat from him. "Go take a shower. I'll get a fire going and make you some coffee." I turned back around to get started on it, but his cold, clammy hand grabbed onto my arm, quickly but gently.

I pivoted to look up at him, waiting for him to say something. But he didn't. He just looked down at me with no words or emotions. "What? Are you hurt?" I ruffled my eyebrows, starting to panic.

"No," he cleared his throat. "I'm not hurt. Just surprised you didn't leave." His eyes turned glossy as he stared at me in shock.

I felt my eyes tear up for the thousandth time today. "Don't do that." I cursed and brushed the tear that was rolling down my face. I broke from his light grip and walked away to start the coffee again.

I had a small fire going in the fireplace and just pulled the coffee from the coffee maker when I heard his footsteps behind me. I grabbed the mug he use to always pick, and poured the black liquid in.

He stood shirtless, with old jeans on, in front of the crackling fireplace. I felt my heart skip a beat. There stood the man I had been convincing myself to hate for the past year. It was easy when I wasn't around him. But where I had to face him, it was a whole other story.

I swallowed hard and walked up to him, holding two mugs.

"Thanks." He took his mug from my hands, his finger tips brushing against them. It gave me butterflies.

"You should really put a shirt on." I mumbled, folding my arm over my chest as I sipped the coffee. It was too hot for me to drink.

"I didn't get that cold." He tried to make a point.

"Yeah, but it's hard to stay mad at you when you're walking around shirt-less."

I let the flirtatious comment slip out. We needed some normalcy between the two of us.

He huffed a little chuckle, his mustache curling up in the process, and shook his head. Then took a drink from the coffee. I smiled a bit and gazed up at him. He glanced down at me and then looked away immediately. "If I can't be shirtless, then you can't look at me like that." He sighed.

I held back a bigger smile and looked down at my feet. "Okay." I whispered and then went to sit down on the couch.

He flipped the radio on, and Cody Johnson filled the room. I curled up on the end of the couch and watched the orange fire dance as Kayce stood by it and watched me. We were silent, as we had been. We didn't know what was happening or what to say. Afraid to say anything, because we might ruin this. Whatever this was.

He finished the coffee and sat the mug down on the end table with a small clatter.

"Do you want more coffee?" I asked.

"Whiskey." He grinned softly. I untangled myself from the couch and started to stand up. "I can get it, baby-" When the word left his lips, he froze. Baby. I also stayed still and sat back down slowly, feeling all the color drain from my face. His mouth hung open a small amount. He struggled to speak and just shook his head at first. "Im sorry, I didn't mean to-"

"It's okay." I forced the words out through my hoarse voice.

He patted my shoulder as he walked by. My skin burned where he had touched. He went into the bedroom and came back out with a tshirt on. Then I heard the kitchen cabinet door open and a glass bottle being pulled from the shelf. He came over and sat on the opposite end of the couch, and watched the fire with me. His arm propped up over the top of the couch causally and the other holding his whiskey on the arm rest. If I could've stayed there forever I would have.

Suddenly, a loud banging on the door made me jump. Kayce looked at me calmly,"It's okay." He nodded but rose to his feet abruptly. The knocking was louder and harder the next time.

"Kayce!" Rip called out from the other side of the door. It put goosebumps on my arms.

Kayce flung the wooden door open. "What's going on?" His tone was no longer calm.

I turned around on the couch and looked over at the door. Rip stared a hole through me. And then at Kayce.

He was holding a long rifle and had mud covering his boots to nearly his knees. His chest was rising and falling quickly. He clenched his jaw when he saw me.

"Ada..." he uttered. "That's... goddammit." He swore.

"What the fuck is going on?" Kayce asked again, hatefully this time.

"There was a guy from Jakes crew in the barn. Said that there's a group of 'em planning to come out here tonight."

Dread overcame me. "No. Not again." I stood from the couch, denying it all.

I blocked out everything they said and went straight to the whiskey cabinet Kayce had just been to. A heavy bottle of Blantons was shoved to the back left corner. The bottle scraped against the shelf and hit the counter with a clink. The lid popped open and I put the bottle to my lips, drinking the dark bitter whiskey.

I put the bottle back and turned to see Kayce putting his boots. A pistol tucked into his jeans behind his back. Rip was no longer in the doorway. I hadn't even heard him walk away. As Kayce put on his black cowboy hat he glanced at me. He immediately looked back, as if he knew what I was about to say. As I opened my mouth, he stopped me.

"I know this isn't the life you want. I know you don't like how I handle things. Or all the fighting. And I get it." He nodded once, showing the confidence in his answer. "But as long as you're here on this earth, I will do anything to keep you safe. And you won't be alone. I know that's gotta mean something to you." His words paralyzed me. He was more than right about every sentence that fell from his lips because I had told him those words years ago when he asked me to live with him and everyone thought we were crazy.

But he didn't give me time to think or react. He snatched the rifle up from the corner. "Get your shoes on. I ain't gonna leave you here." My jaw shook from weakness, but I knew I didn't have much time so I hurried to the bedroom and slipped my boots on. I turned the corner back to the living room as Kayce pulled another pistol out his coat pocket. I looked at it and he looked at me. "Just in case." He whispered and held it out to me.

I swallowed hard. When we first got together, I wouldn't have dared take it. Not after everything I had gotten myself through. I stared at it with fear. My shaky hand reached out and took the cold black metal from him.

"Just in case." I whispered back.